Ski
For Your
Mountain

SHARON SIAMON

illustrations by Brenda Clark

gage PUBLISHING LIMITED
TORONTO ONTARIO CANADA

Canadian Cataloguing in Publication Data

Siamon, Sharon.
    Ski for your mountain

(Jeanpac)
ISBN 0-7715-7007-4

I. Title.   II. Series: Jeanpac paperback original.

PS8587.I25S54   jC813′.54   C83-098209-4
PZ7.S42Sk

DESIGN: Artplus/ Brant Cowie

Printed and bound in Canada by Webcom Limited

To Mom, Morning, Aileen

Acknowledgments: I'd like to thank Pat Hurst of Larder Lake Ski Club, Abe Aidelbaum of Pineland Ski School in Kirkland Lake, and Lori Kreiner of Kamiskotia for sharing their ski lore for this book.

Other Books by Sharon Siamon:

Strange Lake Adventure

A Puli Named Sandor

Contents

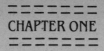
The Top of Snowbird Mountain

"There's nothing to be afraid of," the voice behind April Martineau said firmly. "Just let yourself go!"

April could not move. She did not dare raise her eyes from the blinding white snow under her skis. She had already had one sickening glimpse of the cliff that fell from the top of the ski lift at Snowbird Mountain. The run they called 'The Exterminator'.

She wanted to shut her eyes and shut out that awful view of trees and frozen lakes impossibly far below, but her head spun whenever she closed her eyes. She wanted to close her ears to the swift hiss of skiers passing her and plummeting down the mountain at terrible speed—she was afraid they would swoop her away with them! Her red ski mitts clutched her poles and drove them into the packed snow.

"It's exactly like the hill you've already practised on!" April could hear the impatience rising in her cousin Karen's voice. "We'll just do your turns, nice and wide, and you can follow me down." Karen's voice was ringing in April's ears,

6

but all she heard, all she understood was that Karen was going to leave her alone! Stranded at the top of the hill!

She must try. April forced herself to look — not at the four kilometres of mountain falling away beneath her, but just at the first few metres of it. Karen was gliding away, smoothly and with effortless grace, doing a slow leisurely turn at the right of the run and skiing back across the hill.

She stopped and looked up, shielding her eyes with a mittened hand. "Come on!" Karen's blond bangs were a blaze of light under her blue ski hat. Her blue and white ski suit matched the sky, the endless blue sky behind her. That view of sky made April's legs turn to spaghetti!

In a minute I'm going to faint, she told herself reasonably. If I faint, the ski patrol will have to come up and get me on a stretcher, and if that happens Danny Antoniazzi and *everybody* will know what a terrible coward I am. I've got to *try*! Danny was fourteen, like Karen, and helped run the tow at Snowbird Mountain when he wasn't training with Karen for competition. The two of them were among the best young downhill ski racers in Northern Ontario.

April waited until half a dozen more skiers, some much younger than her eleven years, had whirled away below. Then, pointing her skis, not down, but towards the pines at the right side of the run she slowly let herself slide forward. "Knees bent. . . up. . . turn!" she chanted, the way Karen had taught her. She shifted her weight to her right foot and felt her skis coming around.

At that moment she caught sight of the awful

hill, falling, endlessly falling, below her. She forgot to keep her weight on the right ski and go into a crouch for the next turn. She forgot everything in a moment of total terror. She suddenly found herself flying down the mountain, her skis picking up speed with every second.

"Turn! Turn!" Karen shrieked behind her, but it was too late. April could not turn. She was already skiing much too fast for her level of turning skill.

"Just fall," Karen shouted, taking up her racing stance, crouched low, poles back, "like I showed you, back and sideways... FALL!"

With a mighty dig of her poles, Karen hurtled after her cousin. "FALL, April," she shouted again. "NOW!" But the wind whipped the words from her mouth and April heard nothing but a great roaring in her ears. Ahead yawned the terrible white emptiness of the 'nosedive', where the hill fell straight down for over a hundred metres. A few more ski lengths and she'd be over the edge!

Suddenly, April saw a blinding flash of blue as Karen slipped across her path. And now she heard the shouted advice to fall and wondered why she hadn't thought of it. It seemed so sensible. She felt herself flying through the air as if in slow motion, felt the skis leave her feet as the bindings released on impact, felt the sting of snow in her face and a clumsy clutter of arms and legs that didn't seem to be in the right place at all. Then there was a bright silence, and then the wind blowing through the pines over her head, and Karen's worried face staring into her own.

"Are you okay?"

"I guess so." It was such blissful relief to lie there, pillowed in the soft white snow. Alive! Not falling!

But as April tried to twist in the deep snow and roll over, she felt a hot poker of pain drive through her left shoulder.

"What's the matter?" Karen was quick to notice the spasm of pain that crossed her cousin's face.

"I . . . don't . . . know . . . ," April stammered. She could feel tears stinging behind her eyes. Her whole left side felt like it was on fire.

"Stay here. Don't move." April saw her cousin straighten and ski quickly to the centre of the run, where she waved down the next skier. She heard her shout, "Get the ski patrol up here, fast, with a stretcher. Get Danny."

April sank back into the snow. I might as well have fainted at the top of the mountain, she told herself. Danny's going to know I'm no skier anyway. They're all going to know. I'll never *be* a skier. Alive, but so what? I'll never be part of all this. I'll never be a Hearst!

She had wanted so much to be part of it. Lying there, waiting for the next ski patrol to take her down the mountain, April remembered arriving at Snowbird Mountain two months ago, in October, right after her dad had died. She remembered driving down the last few kilometres of dirt road toward the ski resort in her Uncle Neil and Aunt Nora's gold pick-up. And how right then, right from the beginning, she'd got off on the wrong foot! Or ski, really, thought April ruefully

—you couldn't think of the Hearsts without skis on their feet!

She'd been so anxious to get a glimpse of the mountain. All her life she'd been hearing about Snowbird Mountain in the northeast corner of Ontario. Her father, Michael Martineau, had helped *his* father build the resort, before he'd grown up and moved away to British Columbia. He'd always promised to bring April back to visit the log lodge at the foot of Snowbird Mountain and her aunt and uncle and her cousin Karen. Now she was coming alone.

"There it is!" her Uncle Neil suddenly exclaimed. April saw nothing but a line of lumpy hills along the horizon. It was cloudy, that October day, and for a second April thought that low clouds must be hiding the peaks, the way they often did at home.

"See," Uncle Neil pointed, "that one to the right is Snowbird."

April couldn't believe it! That ordinary looking *hill* — Snowbird Mountain! But then she was from B.C., where a *mountain* was a *mountain*.

As they unloaded the truck in the ski lodge parking lot, April looked around for the chair lifts, a chalet, and above all, the mountain. All she saw was a scrubby brown hill, with scars of matted grass running down through the trees, an old log lodge and two wooden shacks.

"It's so much . . . smaller . . . than Dad said," she blurted in confusion. Instantly, she knew she'd said the wrong thing. Not just any old wrong thing, but the really super wrong one! A shadow passed quickly over the faces of her cousin Karen

11

and her parents, like a cloud passing over the sun.

"She's certainly a Martineau, isn't she?" Uncle Neil said, with an amused glance at Aunt Nora. "Well, I guess it's not a very fancy place, April, but we have plans to build it up." April's Aunt Nora looked embarrassed, and Karen just stalked away toward the lodge. Karen looked very much like her father, tall and lean, with long heavy blond hair.

April remembered how she had felt then, like sinking down through the gravel under her feet. She hadn't meant it the way it sounded. It was just that the whole world seemed to have shrunk since getting off the plane in Timmins. The trees were shorter, the houses seemed smaller, and to call that piddling little molehill a mountain!

Snowbird Mountain has sure got even with me for thinking that way, April thought, wincing at the pain in her shoulder. It looks high enough from the top! She shuddered, thinking of the sickening view from the top of the ski tow. It had seemed higher than anywhere she'd ever been except in an airplane. All she wanted now was to be down, down, down! The pain was getting worse, and she could feel the cold beginning to seep through her red ski suit.

Just then she heard the scrape of ski edges coming to a sudden halt above her. April looked up and saw Danny Antoniazzi and two ski patrollers with their Hessian red jackets and first aid pouches slung around their waists.

"It's April!" Danny's voice cracked with astonishment.

"She's hurt her shoulder. Did you bring a

stretcher? Good!" Karen motioned for the two ski patrollers, Andy and Lise, to bring the stretcher over to where April lay, a small red figure under the trees.

"What happened, Ape?" Danny's brown eyes appeared above April's face, and the name he loved to tease her with brought the first real tears to April's eyes. She waited for Karen to tell Danny how she'd lost her nerve and wiped out on the first turn . . . but Karen was silent. The silence was almost worse than an accusation.

"I guess I kind of . . . lost control . . ." April said finally. "Didn't give it enough edge, I guess." Somehow, it was easier to talk about the edges of her skis than to admit she was afraid, a total coward.

"Never mind, that's lesson two," Danny joked. "We'll have you back up here in no time, eh, Karen?"

April caught the flash of anger in Karen's eyes. She doesn't want to be bothered teaching me to ski, April thought. Maybe she already knows it's a lost cause!

Lise and Andy were rolling her gently onto the stretcher now, wrapping her in a brown wool blanket, and strapping her firmly down. The ski stretcher was built like a sled with a rope on each end. The two expert young skiers could ease it smoothly down the hill between them. It felt very good to April to be securely strapped in, even though the elastic straps hurt her shoulder.

"Just shut your eyes, lie back and enjoy the ride," Danny said. "*This* is the easy way down!"

13

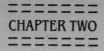

CHAPTER TWO

A Separated Shoulder

With great skill the two ski patrollers brought April down the mountain. Danny and Karen skied ahead to clear a path. April could hear the other skiers on the run call to each other as she passed, bundled up like a mummy on the ski stretcher.

"Who's hurt? . . . Who got hurt?" It was always exciting when the ski patrol went into action. They wore bright red crosses on their packs to identify them, and the sled slung between them with its tightly wrapped bundle was a signal to all skiers that someone had been injured on the hill.

Wait till Uncle Neil and Aunt Nora find out that it's me! April thought. Their own niece! Uncle Neil and Aunt Nora had both been champion skiers themselves, but more than that, they were so proud of their ski school's safety record. No kid had ever been seriously injured learning to ski at Snowbird Mountain. And now, thought April miserably, I come along and wipe out that good record on my first lesson!

It seemed to take forever to get down. By the time they reached the lodge, April's shoulder was feeling every bump and mogul on the hill, no matter how slowly and carefully the ski patrollers tried to guide her sled over them.

At the bottom, Uncle Neil was waiting to unstrap the sled and carry her into the lodge. Like Karen, he didn't say anything. The look in his eyes, April thought, says it all. One *more* thing to worry about!

Aunt Nora was waiting in front of the woodstove fire to help April out of her ski suit. Getting the jacket off was the worst. April gritted her teeth to keep from screaming.

Uncle Neil felt her burning shoulder gently, with experienced hands. "Might be separated," he said. "We'll have to support it with bandages and get her into the hospital at Iroquois Falls."

Aunt Nora's grey eyes flashed angrily at Karen. "What on *earth* were you thinking of . . . taking April to the top on her first day out!"

"She was ready!" Karen said. She was angry too. Don't fight over me, April thought desperately. It was my fault, not Karen's. But Karen went on, "We practised all morning on the novice hill. She was doing fine. She was ready!"

"Obviously she wasn't!" Aunt Nora replied crisply. "Or she wouldn't be lying here with an injured shoulder!"

"She was on short skis," Danny jumped in to defend Karen. "We usually do take our GLM students up to the top the first day if they're doing all right, Mrs. Hearst." GLM stood for *Graduated Length Method*, where the students started out with very short skis and gradually wore longer ones as they developed skill.

"It could happen to anyone." Danny smiled down at April, giving her some badly needed reassurance.

"Well, it shouldn't happen, especially not to one of us!" Aunt Nora retorted. "I appreciate your trying to defend Karen, Danny, but the fact is . . ."

"The fact is, all this isn't helping get April some medical help," Uncle Neil reminded his angry wife. "Which she is going to need tonight if we're not going to risk permanent damage to that left shoulder. Karen, go up and get the quilt off April's bed and some aspirin from the bathroom, please. I'll warm up the truck."

April caught a glimpse of Karen's face as she wheeled away. Her fair cheeks were scarlet. With fury? April wondered.

"Aunt Nora," she said, as her aunt tried to make her comfortable in front of the fire, "it really wasn't Karen's fault. I *was* ready, like she said. I just . . . (now she had to say it, get it over with and *say* it!) . . . lost my nerve, I guess. I was too scared to ski down that hill. It looked . . . " She broke off. The memory of what that long fall of white snow had looked like, swept over her and made her shudder.

Aunt Nora looked surprised. She opened her mouth to say something, and then closed it. "I'll go and make you some hot tea," was all she said, but she smiled at April as though she were trying to understand. Then she went off through the swinging doors to the snack bar kitchen.

April was left with Danny. He was still in his heavy ski boots and tan ski parka. He plopped down in the armchair opposite April's, smiled at her. "Does it hurt much, Ape?" he asked her.

"Not when I sit still. You'd better get back out there in case some other dummy needs rescuing!"

April thought she couldn't stand too much of Danny's sympathy. It was the type of sympathy that made you break down and bawl!

"Listen," Danny said, as he stood up to go. "Stop with that 'dummy' stuff, eh? There's nothing dumb about falling when you ski. I do it all the time. And usually you don't get hurt, either. You just weren't lucky, that's all. It doesn't mean a thing!"

But April knew, as she watched Danny's dark head disappear through the door, that it had been a serious fall. If it weren't for Karen I might have got killed, she thought with horror. She saved my life . . . and got blamed for my mistake . . . no wonder she's mad! April lay back with a sigh, forgetting how much that would hurt her shoulder. She was still seeing stars when Aunt Nora came back in with hot tea in a styrofoam cup.

It was a separated shoulder, just as Uncle Neil had feared. Dr. Johnson, the orthopedic specialist in Iroquois Falls, did some very quick and very painful things to set April's arm back into the shoulder socket out of which it had slipped.

"That's what happens when you fall on an outstretched arm," the doctor said. "Keep her arm in this sling," he told Uncle Neil, tying a wide bandage around April's neck, "and see that she rests this shoulder for at least three weeks. No skiing until Christmas holidays, I'm afraid. We want everything to knit together nicely."

April felt relieved. Three more weeks until everyone knew she was too scared to ever try skiing again!

17

"And speaking of skiing," the doctor said. "How are the conditions shaping up out at Snowbird Mountain for the holiday, Neil? My wife and I were thinking of staying home this Christmas instead of taking our usual trip to Mont Tremblant."

Uncle Neil cleared his throat. Dr. Johnson and his wealthy friends were customers. "Well, we've had early snow this year, so there's a good base," he said slowly. "And of course we'll stay open every day during the school holidays."

"Until dark," the doctor commented, looking up from the notes he'd been making on April's condition. "Any plans for putting in night ski-ing. . . light? That sort of thing?"

"We were hoping," Uncle Neil said quietly, "but it looks like that might have to wait till next year."

"That's right, last year was a disaster for you, wasn't it, with the warm weather in January. I'd forgotten. Well, you've got a nice little hill out there," the doctor continued, standing up to show them out. "A few more improvements, like lights, and maybe a little dance floor," he laughed, wig-gling his hips. "It would be tempting to buy a membership at Snowbird, instead of going all over the place. I hate the darn travelling, you know?"

Uncle Neil nodded, his mouth tight.

On the long drive home, Uncle Neil didn't say much, except to mutter that "some people have a lot more money than is good for them!" April knew his mind was on his own money troubles. That last bad year had almost wiped Snowbird out. Uncle Neil had borrowed money to improve the ski runs, and then, when it hadn't snowed, there *was* no skiing. There had been no money to pay back the bank loan, and hardly enough to get Snowbird back into operation this year. Now, every time something needed repairs, or the tow broke down, Uncle Neil looked a year older. April stared out the truck window at the snow-covered rocks along the highway; they looked like soft white pillows against the starry night sky. Finally the painkillers Dr. Johnson had given April took effect, and she dropped off to sleep.

The crunch of tires on the snow in Snowbird Mountain's parking lot woke April up. "Home," she thought sleepily, trying to sit up. Then she realized where she was—not home with her dad in their apartment in Vancouver—but far off in the Ontario bush, living in a log lodge far from the nearest town. As she climbed stiffly out of the truck and stumbled after her Uncle Neil, up to the warm lighted windows of the lodge, April felt a huge emptiness inside. The big main room of the lodge was shadowed and cold; the log tables were cleared off and ready for the next horde of noisy, thumping skiers. A long snack bar connected the big family kitchen to this public area, but the opening was shut off at night with thick, insulating shutters. A door in the centre wall led to the family living room in the back part of the lodge.

"It's warmer in here," Uncle Neil said, opening the door for her. "Get cozy by the fire, while I tell Nora we're home. I guess they didn't hear the truck!"

"If it's okay," April said sleepily, "I think I'll

19

just go to bed." The pills were making her head spin.

"A good sleep is what you need," Uncle Neil agreed. "You go on, then, and I'll send Karen up with some supper." He waited at the bottom of the circular wooden stairway until April had reached the loft she shared with Karen. "You should try to eat."

"Okay, thanks," April said politely. It was no use thinking that her father would have realized she was too tired to eat, would instead have helped her into bed and tucked her in. Uncle Neil is not my father, and I'm too big to get tucked in, she told herself. I wonder if this is the banister Dad carved out of driftwood himself... She leaned heavily on the carved railing to help pull herself up the last weary steps to bed.

Lying alone in her bed under the high log rafters, April was filled with longing for her father. The new pain throbbed in her shoulder, bringing alive the old one of missing him. How disappointed he would have been that I scrapped out on Snowbird Mountain, April thought. I'll never get the courage to go up on that hill on skis again. I know I won't. When she shut her eyes she still felt as though she were standing at the top of that precipice of endless white snow. She could feel herself falling... falling...

When Karen tiptoed up with a bowl of warm soup and some ham sandwiches, she found April fast asleep, her long chestnut hair spread across the pillow, and her good right arm flung out, as if to stop herself from falling.

CHAPTER THREE

Loft and Lodge

April spent the next three weeks with her arm bandaged tightly to her side. She had to get used to doing everything with one arm, which was hard when you were clumsy with two!

While April's shoulder slowly healed, and the Christmas holidays grew closer, one snowstorm after another swept over Northern Ontario. Great snow drifts soon draped the shoulders of Snowbird Mountain.

"Dad always said the snow was beautiful here," April said to Aunt Nora one morning as they stepped outside to find everything sparkling and white. "He was right!"

"Did Michael . . . did your father talk much about Snowbird?" Aunt Nora asked, surprised.

"All the time! He always said we'd take a trip back here so I could see Snowbird Mountain in the winter . . . but we never had enough money, I guess." April shrugged.

"Well, I'm not surprised!" Aunt Nora said. "The way you lived! Always changing jobs and moving around. But it's nice to know he still remembered this old place."

April kicked the snow with her boot. "He loved it," she said. "He told me the best part of himself went into building Snowbird."

"Yes, I can still see him," Aunt Nora nodded, looking up at the lodge. "My easy-going little brother, working for once! Sitting on the top log and swinging a hammer with all his might . . ." She stopped and reached for April's mittened hand. "I'm sorry, April," she said. "Sometimes I forget."

"That's okay, Aunt Nora," April said quickly. "I like to talk about Dad."

She gave Aunt Nora's hand a squeeze. It was something they shared—that habit of talking without thinking first. She had really begun to love her fiery, energetic aunt, even though she was so different from Dad. Uncle Neil was easy to love too, with his quiet strong face; and Karen, April admired with all her heart. If only she could really feel that she belonged here.

Just then Karen came out the front door, her knapsack of books on her back. She glanced at April and her mother, standing hand in hand, and flicked her hair over her shoulder. "C'mon, if you're coming," she said to April. "We're going to miss the bus!"

Karen's voice often has that sharp sound these days, April thought, letting go of her aunt's hand and following her cousin. Ever since Karen got blamed for my fall she's been acting like she wished I would dry up and blow away!

"Last week of school!" Aunt Nora called after them.

April saw Karen's face lighten up as she turned

back to her mother. "And then we *ski* for two whole weeks!" she cried.

Oh boy, April thought. You ski. *I* sleep!

April woke up Thursday morning to find Karen pulling on her best duofold ski underwear. Ski underwear? she thought sleepily. Then the glorious realization hit. This is it—the first day of holidays! Karen's going skiing—I can sleep.

Just then Aunt Nora poked her head up into the loft. "Everybody up?" she asked. "It's a perfect day. In two hours this place will be mobbed with skiers. April! Breakfast in ten minutes!"

So much for sleeping in, April groaned.

"Mother!" called Karen from the other end of the loft, "come up here a minute."

Aunt Nora took a couple more steps up the circular stairs.

"Look at this mess!" Karen gestured around the long narrow loft. Her bed was shoved as far to one end as it would go; April's was at the other. In between stretched a no-man's land strewn with the clothes April had worn that week—sweaters, jeans, socks.

"And my *towel*!" shouted Karen, diving for a damp white object. "Honestly, I can't stand this!"

Nora shook her auburn head at April.

"I was going to clean it up, today..." April started.

"I can't live in this pigsty!" Karen interrupted, flinging April's clothes towards her end. "It's not fair—I keep my stuff neat."

That was certainly true, April thought, ducking a flying green sweatshirt. Karen's side looked

like a TV kid's room — with its terrific ski posters on the wall and the bed always made.

"I've got an idea," Aunt Nora said, coming up the rest of the stairs. "We'll hang up that old green blanket across the loft and make two rooms. Then each of you can have privacy! Now...PEACE!" She caught the last sweater Karen threw and draped it around April's damaged shoulder. "You will have to try being tidier," she told her niece. "Karen isn't used to sharing her space."

"And Karen..." Aunt Nora shook a warning finger at her stormy daughter. "You'll have to realize that being tidy is new for April." There was a look of half laughter and half pity in her eyes. "I'll never forget your apartment in Vancouver," she sighed, sitting on the bed beside April. "There were books and plants and junk *everywhere* . . . and no bills paid, no money in the bank account, no will, not even an address for your mother." She shook her head at the memory. "I don't know how Michael could leave things in such a mess."

April wanted to protest that her father hadn't meant to *leave* anything. He'd called April from the doctor's office after school one day, to say he had a bad headache and the doctor wanted him in the hospital for tests. "I'll see you tomorrow," he'd told her. "Can you manage with Kraft dinner for supper tonight?"

That was the last time April had heard his voice. He'd gone into a sudden coma shortly after he called, and died that night in the hospital, without ever waking up. The next thing April remembered clearly was Aunt Nora arriving

25

like a tiny, auburn-haired tornado, cleaning everything up, packing, and getting April ready to come back with her to Ontario.

April had been too numb with grief and shock to try to save anything from Aunt Nora's quick broom. Her aunt totally disapproved of their way of life —of the collection of great old hats from the Salvation Army, their piles of driftwood collected from ocean beaches, the magazines and photographs and letters and books piled in boxes.

As for her mother —all April knew about her was that she had drifted out of their lives when April was a baby. They didn't have an address because her mother hadn't written in ten years. April and her dad had never missed her.

Aunt Nora, April thought, would never understand the fun they'd had, just she and Dad, living in that messy apartment. It was such a different life from Snowbird Mountain. But I'm here now, she thought, and as Dad would say, "I'd better straighten up and fly right!"

"I'm sorry. I will try to do better. I'll clean up before breakfast," she promised.

Karen had really done most of the work for her. April shoved into a cupboard the pile of clothes Karen had thrown at her. She made the bed as well as she could with one arm and hurried downstairs.

Terrific smells were coming from the kitchen. April had never tasted anything as good as the breakfasts at Snowbird Mountain. Uncle Neil was the chef. As she hopped up on a stool at the snack bar, he heaped her plate with golden French toast with real maple syrup and curly strips of crisp bacon. I'm getting fat eating all this, but it's so good! she thought.

"I'll need Nora and Karen on the hill with me to run and get the ski tow started," Uncle Neil said. "April, can you hold down the kitchen and snack bar?"

"What do I have to do?" April asked.

"Just keep tossing wood in the cookstove and keep the pots of chili and hot dogs warm. Once the skiers get here, one of us will come in to help in the snack bar. You'll need it!"

April grinned at her uncle and nodded. He had a way of talking to you that made you feel grown-up and important.

"Danny'll be here soon," said her aunt, coming to perch on the stool next to April with her plate. "He and Karen can take turns giving you a hand."

Danny's coming! April thought, feeling happy. She hadn't seen much of him since her fall.

"Don't forget Danny and I have to train!" Karen protested from the other end of the snack bar. "It's only three weeks till the first Challenge Cup race at Timmins."

"Nobody's forgetting your ski race," Uncle Neil said briskly. "But you and Danny have had a good start at training, thanks to the early snow. This holiday is important to Snowbird's business. It's going to have to be *work* as well as skiing!"

"Work okay, but not babysitting the snack bar!" fumed Karen. "What about Mrs. Cameron? She always ran the snack bar before."

"We just can't afford extra help this year," Uncle Neil shook his head. "It's going to have to be a family effort." He placed a big hand on his daughter's shoulder. "Let's get out and groom that hill—get ready for the crowd we're going to have today."

Karen sighed, shrugged, and finally shoved back her plate and went to get her coat.

"Sure you'll be all right here for awhile by yourself?" Uncle Neil asked April, as he put on his big parka.

"Sure," April grinned. "I'll just keep the hot dogs hot, and the chili. . .chilly!"

Uncle Neil groaned, "Where did you learn to make jokes that bad, at such a tender age?"

CHAPTER FOUR

Blue Suit and Beige Suit

========================

By nine-thirty, the skiers had started to arrive. As she stoked the stoves and heated water, April heard the lodge fill up with laughter and talk and the clomp of heavy ski boots. Outside, the tow engine hummed to life.

April knew she was supposed to have the snack bar shutters open to serve food by ten and she was glad when Danny came stomping in the kitchen door at quarter to. "Boy, that's getting cold," he told April, stripping off his gloves and blowing on his fingertips.

"Did you have to wait a long time for a ride?" April asked. She knew there wasn't much traffic on the highway between Iroquois Falls and the Snowbird Mountain Road, and Danny always hitchhiked the thirty kilometres to save money.

"Too long, at fifteen below zero!" Danny grinned. He started to push back the shutters that closed off the kitchen from the lodge. "But I finally got a lift with a grocery truck going to Timmins. They're not supposed to take riders, but this guy usually takes pity on me. Well, speaking of pity, how's the shoulder?"

"It's almost better," said April. "Want something to eat?"

"Since when did you get promoted to cook around here?" Danny laughed, coming over to the cookstove. "That's my job, Ape."

"Since I hurt my shoulder and can't wash dishes," April teased back. "I guess you'll have to do them!"

Danny made a face. "Oh no! When did the doc say you'd be able to wash . . . I mean, take off that sling?"

"Two more days," April grinned. "Hot dog or chili?"

Danny lifted the lids and sniffed the pots, one by one. "Doesn't smell too awful," he said. "I might take a chance on a hot dog. I mean, what can you do to a hot dog?"

"Bury it in ketchup, like you do!" said April, handing him a couple of buns from the warming oven above the stove.

"Hey, you manage pretty well with one arm," Danny said, surprised. "Too bad you can't get out there and ski, eh?"

"Never mind. I'm happy here."

"I'd go crazy if I had to stay inside on a day like this!" Danny motioned towards the sun-filled lodge windows. "I wish it would warm up a bit though. Pretty cold at the top of the hill when the wind blows."

"But Aunt Nora said it was perfect," exclaimed April. "Who'd want to ski if it's that cold?" She knew immediately that she'd made another of those 'stupid kid from Vancouver' remarks. Danny was looking at her with a sort of crooked grin. "It couldn't stay this cold all week, could it?" she finished lamely.

"Let's hope not," Danny said, pouring ketchup on his hot dog. "And let's hope it doesn't fall to thirty and forty below, either!" He took a big bite. "Well, are we ready to open for business? Why don't you work out a system for washing dishes with one arm, Ape? Might come in handy."

"Handy for you!" April said. "Listen, this sore shoulder might be the best thing that ever happened to me." She was glad her dumb remark about the cold had been brushed over so quickly. All these people were so touchy about the weather—and anything to do with skiing—it was their whole world. April sighed. It was never that way with Dad. You didn't have to watch what you said every second.

Just then Karen came bustling in the door, cheeks rosy with cold and exercise. She gave Danny a warm smile of welcome. "Dad needs you to run the tow while he runs the rake over the hill," she told him. "The wind's packing it too hard at the top. And you..." she shrugged at April, "Mom said you were supposed to go out and get some fresh air. Maybe you can give her a hand in the ski shack selling tow tickets. It's too cold to just stand around..." She glanced at April's shoulder.

April struggled into her parka and stepped outside. The cold pounced on her like an animal, making her gasp and blink. She pulled her hat down over her ears and looked around in amazement. Lonely old Snowbird looks so busy and proud, she thought, with all these cars and people. The snow bristled with upright skis, and the racks to one side of the door were full. April shaded her eyes and watched the skiers come swooping down the last few metres of hill and take their place in the tow line.

Suddenly, she felt a sharp poke in her sore shoulder! It sent a spike of pain running up her neck and she turned sharply around. A tall man, with his ski poles slung over his shoulder, had caught her with the top of one. She clenched her teeth with the pain and waited for him to apologize. He turned casually from his companion, another tall man in a blue ski suit. He looked blankly at April, as though she weren't there, and then went back to his conversation.

April rubbed her shoulder and watched them move someone else's skis aside in the rack, and put their own, very expensive-looking gear, in its place. Of all the colossal nerve! April thought angrily. The two men were still talking. They had smooth tanned faces and carefully cut hair, like the businessmen April had often seen in downtown Vancouver. They look rich, April thought, but what awful manners!

The two men went into the lodge to put on their boots. In a few minutes they came out again. April saw them pause in the doorway and heard one of them say something to the other about the log walls. She saw him dig his fingernail into the caulking between the logs, take out a large chunk and toss it into the snow. Of all the nerve! she thought again. How dare they act like that!

Everybody else, Uncle Neil, Aunt Nora and

Danny were busy, and in fact all of the other skiers were having too good a time to notice a couple of strangers in expensive ski suits. The two men snapped their boots into new-looking skis and shoved expertly off toward the tow line, all the time gesturing toward the hill and talking earnestly. April thought she would go in and see if Karen had noticed anything strange about them.

But Karen was too busy serving French fries and hot dogs to a long line of little boys. "I don't know how they ski with all this garbage in their stomachs," she whispered to April, "but it's good for business!"

"I'll help," April said, lifting the basket of fries out of the hot oil.

"Are you sure? You've only been out for ten minutes."

"Sure. There's not much to do out there if you're not on skis..." April said, trying to say it lightly.

"I'm sorry about your shoulder..." It was the first time Karen had said that.

"It doesn't matter. Karen, do you know those two tall men that were just in here? The one in the beige suit, and the one in the blue suit?"

"Those fancy one-piece suits you mean?" Karen asked. "No, I never saw either of them. Why?"

"I just wondered. I thought they might be friends, or something..." April said. Good friends might take such a personal interest in the chinking between the logs, she supposed.

"Nope, I don't know them," Karen said. "We get lots of visitors during the holidays. One year

33

we had a bunch of famous hockey players, friends of a guy from Iroquois Falls who played for Los Angeles. They were all good skiers too!"

"Visitors . . . that must be it," April said. They had seemed so interested in Snowbird Mountain; maybe it was the first time they'd skied there.

April took over the line of little boys. They were slow in making up their minds what they wanted, and she no sooner got to the end of the line than the first one was back wanting a chocolate bar. April wanted to make a crack about them just standing there and eating, but as Karen said, it was good for business.

"Do you want a Snackers Bar with peanut butter between crispy wafers," she asked, "or a rich dark chocolate Dream Bar, with caramel oozing inside? Or one of these frothy ones with whipped peppermint milk chocolate?" The six little boys were all staring at her with open eyes and chewing mouths, and she had to admit she was even making herself hungry. They all bought chocolate bars.

Then she saw the door of the chalet open and Aunt Nora come in with the two strange men.

"Will you take over the ski shack?" she asked Karen. "April can manage alone in here."

Aunt Nora looked tiny between the two tall men, but she was walking very straight, with her head thrown back. I wonder what they want, April thought. Aunt Nora was leading them into the family living room, and April noticed that they didn't bother to dust the snow off their boots as they followed her in. Real gentlemen! she thought disgustedly.

There was a short silence, while April burned with curiosity, and then the connecting door between the kitchen and the living room opened.

"April, would you bring us three coffees, regular, please?" her aunt asked. "Right away?" Those last two words told April that her aunt was nervous about having the two men in her living room. She decided to put the coffee in the family's mugs and not the styrofoam cups. She quickly loaded up the tray and hugged it against her with her good arm.

Her Aunt Nora was sitting perched near the front of one of the easy chairs. The tall man in blue was leaning against the brick of the fireplace, and the one in beige was leaning back comfortably in the other easy chair. Inside, their faces looked even more tanned. But somehow, April thought, it isn't a healthy-looking tan. I'll bet it comes out of a bottle.

"So this is your daughter?" the man in blue said.

"No, my niece," Aunt Nora said shortly, not even telling him April's name. Something is wrong here, April thought.

"Well. A real *family* business, isn't that nice . . ." the tall man said. Aunt Nora didn't smile, and April knew she wanted her to go back to the kitchen before she said anything more. But somehow, April didn't want to go. She left the connecting door to the living room open a crack, and stood near the deep-fryer so she could hear the voices through the crack. It was hard to catch the whole conversation, but she could hear snatches.

"An excellent hill, Mrs. Hearst...a lot of potential to be a first class ski resort..."

"Representing an international tourism firm...interested in investing large sums... European tourists are finding Canada more attractive...we can bring them in by the planeload..."

There was more that April didn't catch, but she did hear her aunt's voice, plainly and clearly. "Snowbird Mountain is not for sale, gentlemen."

And then more male voices. "Competition would put you out of business. You don't have the capital to keep going. All we want to do is make an appointment with your husband for sometime next week, after Christmas."

"You might as well make your offer to me!" April heard her aunt say coldly. "We own Snowbird Mountain jointly, so the offer will have to be put to me in any case." The two men insisted that they wanted to talk to the man of the house. They sure don't know Aunt Nora, April thought. She must be steaming mad!

There was a lot more technical talk, all very smooth and official sounding, that April couldn't understand, and one more thing that she could! "We hear you have an excellent ski school. We'd like to move the school to the new complex; you and your husband would have all the resources to train young skiers for the national Olympic team."

"That's exactly what we are doing now at Snowbird," April heard her aunt say. April put her eye to the crack in the door and saw her Aunt Nora standing, facing the two men. "And we don't need fancy chalets and snow-making equipment to do it! You can't make champions with money, gentlemen." Aunt Nora looked cool, but very angry, April thought.

The man in blue, the one who'd picked at the wall, turned to leave. "We'll be back," he said shortly, "after you've had time to mull all this over. In the meantime, you'll be reading the details of our plans in the local and national newspapers. This ski resort is to be the biggest thing that has happened to this area since the gold rush."

April saw that they were moving towards the door, and quickly stepped back. The man in the beige ski suit smiled at her in a fake friendly way as he passed, but April gave him her coldest stare in return. Whoever these men were, she was now sure, they were no friends of Snowbird Mountain!

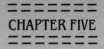

CHAPTER FIVE

A Christmas Blizzard

Just how unfriendly they were, April had to wait until after dinner to find out. They were all sitting in front of the fire in the living room that night when Aunt Nora suddenly said quietly, "Maybe this is a good time to tell you..."

"Tell us what?" said Uncle Neil sleepily from the depths of his easy chair. It had been a long, busy day at Snowbird Mountain.

"I mean, I wish I didn't have to bother you with it, Neil...it's nothing, really...but they said they'd be back!"

"Who said? What on earth are you talking about, Nora?" Uncle Neil sat up in his chair.

"Two men, representing a large company with a lot of money. Millions of dollars, they said. They want to build a great, big year-round resort."

"Oh?" said Uncle Neil, suddenly interested. "Where?"

"Here! They want our property on the south face of Snowbird Mountain for their ski lifts, and they want to buy the lodge. They say if we don't sell, they'll put us out of business anyway! They came this afternoon."

Uncle Neil looked very serious. He didn't move. "What did you tell them?" he said slowly.

"I told them Snowbird was not for sale. Ever. At any price. I said we've always had plans for expanding on the south face of Snowbird ourselves."

Uncle Neil pounded the arm of his chair. April saw Danny and Karen exchange alarmed glances. "If only!" Uncle Neil said. "If only we hadn't lost so much money last year! Our position at the bank is so shaky."

"But we don't have to sell," Aunt Nora said quietly.

"No," agreed Uncle Neil, hesitantly.

"You'd never sell Snowbird!" Karen cried, looking horrified at the thought.

"Those big companies always talk about moving in and doing things in a big way . . ." Danny said. "A million dollars here, a million there. Most of the time it's just hot air, Mr. Hearst."

"Maybe . . ." Uncle Neil said.

"Danny's right," Aunt Nora sighed. "But the way they talk, honestly, you'd think the ski runs were already groomed, the guest chalets were already built, the planeloads of tourists were on their way!"

"And they represent a lot of power . . . not just money," Uncle Neil added. "They talk that way because they know they have the power to make it happen. Not like us. If they really need our land . . ." He stopped and just gazed into the fire.

April knew he was really worried.

"But we'll be back on our feet after this year," Aunt Nora cried. "Look at that crowd we had today! Things will look different, Neil, once we start to pay that bank loan off. All we need is one good year — and we've got it. The weather's perfect."

But Aunt Nora was wrong about the weather. By the time Uncle Neil had to drive Danny home at ten, the temperature had fallen to thirty below zero.

That night the wind howled around Snowbird Mountain, and drove frost through the window cracks in the loft. When April woke up on Christmas Eve, the room was icy cold. She snuggled deeper under her quilts, listening to Karen stamping around on the other side of the blanket wall.

"Well, that's it for skiing!" Karen came swishing through the blanket. "You can't see a thing outside, and it's forty-three below! I'll bet the roads are closed, and Dad doesn't even start the tow!" Her face was a mask of despair.

April wiggled her toes in the warm bed and wondered again why anyone would be crazy enough to ski at forty-three below zero!

Downstairs, all the woodstoves were blazing, and warmth was slowly spreading to the corners of the big, chilly lodge.

"Karen, chuck another log in the living room stove, will you, please?" Aunt Nora asked as they came into the kitchen. "I've got my hands full here!" She wiped a smudge of soot from her nose.

"Where's Uncle Neil?" April asked.

"Out looking for a Christmas tree," Aunt Nora said. "After all, it *is* Christmas Eve!"

Karen scraped a patch of ice off the kitchen window and peered out. "I hope he makes it back," she cried. "Look at the drifts behind the lodge!"

Just then the door flew open and in blew a lot of snow, a lot of pine tree, and Uncle Neil. "Here's our tree," he puffed, "but nobody else sets foot outside the lodge today, do you hear? It's a full scale blizzard!"

So Snowbird Mountain didn't open, as Karen had predicted. The sturdy log lodge at the foot of the mountain rode out the storm for the next two days like a big ship lost in the swirling snow and wind. April tried not to think of other Christmases, in Vancouver. She and her dad always walked to Stanley Park on Christmas Day, and brought Christmas greetings to the animals, and wished there were snow. And now, it seemed as though there were nothing in the whole world except snow!

Christmas morning they ate cinnamon bread hot from the cookstove oven, and listened to carols on the radio while they opened presents. The living room was cozy, with its popcorn strung tree, and the firelight dancing on the log walls. But outside the wind still howled, and the window panes were thick with ice.

April had made her presents in craft class at school: a key chain for Uncle Neil, woven pin baskets for Aunt Nora and Karen. She received new pyjamas and a new blue sweater, and beautiful pony-tail holders from Karen. But the best Christmas present of all was taking off her arm sling.

"Now you'll be able to shovel with both arms," Uncle Neil teased. "We'll need you. It's going to take us a week to dig ourselves out."

"If it ever stops snowing!" wailed Karen. "Listen to that wind."

"How does your shoulder feel, April?" Aunt Nora asked.

"Great!" April grinned. Her arm was a little stiff, but otherwise it felt perfectly normal. Two arms — at last!

CHAPTER SIX

Boxing Day Battles

===========================

The next day, Sunday, was Boxing Day. The snow stopped, and the world outside the iced-up lodge windows was hushed and still.

"Minus 35—too cold really to ski—but I'm going to plough the road and start the tow in case someone turns up," Uncle Neil said at breakfast. The excitement of Christmas had pushed back the shadow of Snowbird Mountain's money problems, and the visit of the two businessmen; but today, April thought, you can really see how worried Uncle Neil has been about losing business on account of the storm.

Uncle Neil fished a long envelope out of his plaid shirt pocket. "I've been looking at these entry forms for the Challenge Cup," he said. "They've raised the fee this year to fifty dollars for each skier for each race. That, plus travelling and food and motels...racing's going to cost us a bundle."

Karen sat up quickly. "But I have to enter!" she cried. "There's no chance of getting on the Northern Ontario team if I don't win those races."

Aunt Nora shook her head. "I suppose we should be focussing all our effort on Karen, and

43

dropping Danny from our plans," she said. "Unless his parents could help."

Karen stood up in one swift movement and faced her mother with a blazing face. "Drop Danny!" she cried. "We've always raced together. I can't do it without Danny!"

Aunt Nora was about to reply angrily, when Uncle Neil cut in. "I think Danny has earned his place, Nora," he said. "And this is his last chance to make the Divisional team. Next year they'll probably think he's too old."

"I know all that," said Aunt Nora, "but . . ."

"I won't do it without Danny," Karen said, and April suddenly realized her cousin was close to tears. "I won't go to one single race." She turned away and sped up the loft stairs.

April quietly wandered out to the kitchen to fix herself another piece of peanut butter on toast. Ever since she'd hurt her arm, she'd been eating whenever she felt miserable. Like now. The more the Hearsts talked about the shortage of money the hungrier she got.

"I know I shouldn't eat you," she said to the peanut butter on toast, holding it up in front of her. "I've just had breakfast and Karen will nag me about getting fat. I'll be sorry I took even one bite!" She reached for the jar and smeared an extra thick gob of peanut butter on top of one corner of the sandwich. "Especially this first bite . . ." she said, stuffing it into her mouth. "Mmmmm." For a few minutes she felt better. But then the toast was gone, and the emptiness inside came back. In Vancouver I didn't even like peanut butter, April thought, reaching for the

44

knife with one hand and the loaf of bread with the other.

There was a sudden tap at the door that made her jump. Danny's face appeared through the thick frost, and April jumped up to let him in.

"Hello!" she cried, delighted to see his friendly face. "I didn't think you'd come today. It's still so cold."

"Got a ride with some relatives going to Timmins for a big family blow-out," Danny said. "The wind's stopped, so I thought we might open. I also brought this." He took a rolled-up newspaper out from under his parka, and spread it on the counter. "Is this one of the guys you saw on Thursday?"

"That's him!" April cried. "That's Blue Suit! Does it say his name?"

"A. M. Delorac," Danny read. "Representative of a company that is planning a multi-million ski and summer resort at nearby Snowbird Mountain. They don't give the name of the company. It all sounds crazy!"

April shook her head. "In B.C. we had lots of big ski developments like they're talking about. It doesn't sound crazy to me."

"Oh, in the Rocky Mountains, sure," laughed Danny. "What I wouldn't give to ski out there! But up here in the middle of the bush? Who's going to come?"

"Lots of people would like it," April said. "It's beautiful, and wild, and. . ."

"You think so?" Danny looked surprised. "Karen said you kind of looked down your nose at our north country."

"That was just at first," April said quickly.

"When I first got here, I was so surprised. It just wasn't what I had expected. Now I think it's beautiful."

"Except during a blizzard, eh?" Danny reached over and ruffled her smooth hair. "Hey!" he cried. "You've got your bandage off."

"You noticed," April grinned.

Suddenly, Karen came swinging through the door to the living room. She glared at Danny.

"What are you doing in here?" she demanded. "Dad's starting the tow!"

April couldn't believe it. Five minutes ago Karen had been defending Danny with her life. Now when she was facing him, her eyes were shooting daggers.

Danny hastily folded up the newspaper. "Sure, let's go!" he said. "Coming, Ape? Why don't I show you how to cross-country ski today? It'll loosen up that shoulder and keep you warm out there."

"Well, you two can play around on cross-country skis if you want," Karen said. "I'm going up the tow. We've got some training for the Challenge Cup to do, in case you've forgotten!"

"Forgotten..." Danny started to say, but Karen flung past them, banging the kitchen door on the way out.

"I guess she's right," Danny shrugged. "Your uncle's not going to keep the tow open long if nobody shows up. I'd better get some runs in now." He pulled on his ski gloves. "We'll just postpone that lesson."

"Postpone it permanently," April said. "I'm staying off skis for the rest of my life!"

"Nah, you'll love cross-country," Danny grinned wickedly as he went out. "No hills, Ape!"

April hurried into her parka and followed him outside. At first, the bright sun on the pure white snow made her eyes squeeze shut with sudden tears. When she got used to the light, April saw that amazing things had happened to Snowbird during the two-day blizzard. The lodge was half buried in a sea of snowdrifts. Each curling drift looked like a huge wave about to topple over, but frozen in mid-air. Each tree stood in its own perfect whirlpool of snow. There was not a breath of wind, and it was as if all the wild blowing motion of the storm had suddenly been frozen still. Nothing moved except the long line of T-bars from the tow shack up to the top of Snowbird Mountain.

Suddenly, April saw two skiers shoot over the lip of the nosedive. It was Karen and Danny. Together they carved two perfect S-curves down Snowbird, two perfect plumes of snow high in the air behind them. April sucked in a deep breath of cold air. It was the most beautiful thing she'd ever seen. I wish . . . she thought — no, what's the use! I'll never be able to do that!

By 11:00 that morning no one had come, and Uncle Neil decided to close Snowbird for the day.

"Please Dad, don't close the tow," Karen pleaded. She was yelling over the whining of the tow engine, and when it shut down her voice suddenly sounded very loud against the silence. "Please Dad, if I have to quit now, the whole day will be wasted!"

"It's too expensive to keep all this machinery

running for two skiers, even if they are champions," Uncle Neil said. "And anyway, it's too cold for you as well. I don't want you and Danny risking frostbite. It's darn near thirty below again!"

Karen turned away in disgust, and April wondered how her cousin could be so selfish. It's not as if Uncle Neil wants to shut down the tow, April thought. All Karen thinks about is herself.

Danny came sweeping up to the tow shack and stopped in a shower of snow. "I checked the tow mechanism up top, Mr. Hearst," he said. "Everything's okay." He stepped out of his ski bindings and picked up his skis. "C'mon, Ape. Let's go inside and warm up. My cheeks are feeling numb."

Karen stomped up to them as Danny was standing his skis in the rack. She was white-faced with cold and disappointment.

"Hey Karen," Danny said, "did your Dad say if he wanted me to stay over tonight? Are we opening tomorrow?"

"I want you to stay," April blurted. "It's boring when you're not around." As soon as the words were off her lips, she could have bitten off her tongue. Karen's white face turned scarlet with anger.

"Oh yes, you like having Danny around, don't you?" she said, her words blistering with sarcasm. "He's so much more *interesting* than we are. Maybe if you get off your fat bottom and did some skiing, instead of just watching Danny go up and down the hill, you wouldn't find it so *boring* around here!" She flung her precious racing skis

down into the snow and strode off to the lodge.

Danny bent down to pick the skis up. "Hey, what's the matter with Karen?" he asked in genuine alarm. "I mean, I know she's mad about the tow closing, but that's not your fault. Aren't you two getting along, Ape?"

"I guess . . . not," April stammered, too choked with emotion to talk. She wanted to run, fly, blow away with the snow — anything to get away from here!

"That's too bad," Danny sympathized. "Let's get inside, you're freezing." He took hold of her arm and pulled her after him into the warmth of the lodge. Thankfully, no one else was there. April plunked down on one of the picnic benches and tried not to look as miserable as she felt.

"Look, I know what it's like to be the odd-person-out in a family," Danny said. "Guess why I spend all my time over here? I started hitchhiking over to Snowbird when I was nine and my dad wanted to put me on a hockey team. I hate hockey! Your uncle and aunt kind of adopted me, and I've been coming here ever since. At home they think I'm a weirdo. They can't understand why I'd give up hockey and work for nothing, just to have a chance to ski. When I'm home everybody just sort of stares at me! Danny the freak!"

"Well, that's what I am here!" April cried, her anger rising. "April, the fat freak! I can't ski, I don't want to ski, I hate skiing!" She felt herself wanting to scream it at the top of her lungs, I HATE SKIING!

"Hey, April, get hold of yourself," Danny whispered quickly, grabbing both of her shaking hands in his own. "You've never even given skiing a chance."

"Did you give hockey a chance?" April whispered back fiercely. "I do know I hate it. One fall was enough for me. I don't need to do it again." But his hands steadied her. She slowly got past the screaming stage.

Danny grinned. "Are you going to give Karen the satisfaction . . ." He stopped as the door to the living room opened and Karen came through. She held her chin high and didn't look at them as she said, "Dad says the forecast is for more cold and we probably won't open, so you might as well not stay. If things are better tomorrow, we'll call you."

"Too bad about our training," Danny said. "But we'll make it up, don't worry."

"*You* don't care if we do or not!" Karen said, and quickly turned away, banging the living room door behind her.

"What's the matter with her?" Danny asked again. "I've never seen her like this before."

"It's simple," said April, staring after Karen. "She hates me."

"Nah, she doesn't hate you." Danny stood up and looked around the big empty lodge. "I know what's wrong. You've all been shut in this place, away from everybody else, and Karen's going crazy without skiing. It's too bad she won't come cross-country with us."

"With us?" said April, astonished. "Are you crazy? I told you, I DON'T WANT TO SKI. And it's almost thirty below out there!"

"It's a lot warmer in the bush. And cross-

51

country's more like walking than skiing. It'll be good for you—get you in shape."

"You sound just like the rest of them. So I'm out of shape. So what!" April was almost in tears again.

"I didn't mean that. Listen, April . . ." Danny sat down beside her again. "It'll do you good to get out of here. You need to do your own thing for awhile."

April stared at him, suddenly realizing what Danny was offering her. A chance to get away, out of sight of the ski hill, and Karen. A chance to be alone. Anything was better than being stuck in Snowbird Lodge right now.

"Okay," she said quickly.

"Okay?" asked Danny, caught off guard by April's sudden agreement. "Did you say *okay*?"

"You convinced me. Let's go cross-country skiing." And let's get it over with before I change my mind, she thought.

"All *right*!" Danny cheered. "Here," he said, handing her an awkward bundle of skis and ski poles from the tall cupboard near the door. "Hold these while I get some boots for us and tell your aunt we're going."

Once outside, April wondered if it were all a big mistake. "I'm freezing!" she told Danny. "These thin little boots aren't going to keep my feet warm. And how do you keep these long skinny skis from getting tangled up?"

"It's easy," Danny said, showing her how to snap the binding on the toe of her boot. "Now just grip your pole like this . . . and follow me." He took a few long gliding steps and stopped to let her catch up. "That's it," he grinned. "You're a natural! Just plant your pole beside your instep, now step...and glide." A few more easy strides and they were at the entrance to the trail.

"We'll just do the beginner's loop," Danny called to her. "It takes about an hour. All the trails are big loops that lead back to the lodge, so if you ever feel lost just keep to the left and you'll get back here."

An hour later, they emerged from the bush at the same spot. April's hair was sticking out of her hat in two frozen tufts, but she was warm inside her ski suit, and her feet were positively hot!

"Well?" called Danny, as they skied up to the lodge. "How did you like it?"

April nodded and smiled a big smile. She had to admit cross-country wasn't hard, didn't *seem* dangerous, and kept you amazingly warm. But the best thing of all was the wonderful feeling of freedom that she'd had in the bush. It was a magical world out there along the trail, and now April felt she could escape to it whenever she wanted to. She wouldn't need a tow, or perfect weather, or any of those things downhill skiing depended on. She could just put on her skis and go.

Aunt Nora greeted them at the door. "Good news!" she called. "The forecast is for fine weather tomorrow and we'll be open. Can you stay over, Danny? I've got lasagna for dinner."

"*Mais oui*," Danny said. "I don't know which is better news, the weather, or the lasagna!"

Inside the lodge, the smell of baked lasagna was heavenly, and April quickly stowed away the ski gear and went to set the table. As she set plates and silverware on the woven yellow placemats, she heard quick footsteps on the circular stairs and looked up to see Karen. "Look at the little helper..." April heard Karen mutter sarcastically as she went past on her way to the kitchen.

I'd like to wring her long, skinny neck! thought April, twisting the placemat in her hand. The warm feeling inside evaporated, and even though the lasagna was delicious, and Danny teased and joked at dinner, April felt miserable. She ate twice as much as she really wanted, and her stomach felt so full she reached under the table to undo her jeans button.

"What's the matter?" asked Karen innocently from across the table. "Pants getting too tight, April?"

"No," lied April, "they're fine." She'd throw up, she thought, before she'd undo those jeans now.

Danny threw her an affectionate grin. "She just likes to eat good cooking, don't you, Ape?"

"She just likes to eat... period," said Karen under her breath.

April's knuckles tightened on the edge of the table. I'd like to throw this lasagna right in that smug, sarcastic face of yours! April thought furiously. It didn't help that what Karen said was true!

"If everybody's finished," Aunt Nora said quickly, "I'd like to clear the table and get to work with the racing schedules. We've lost some training time and we're going to have to double up."

"April and I will do the dishes," said Uncle

Neil, standing up. He'd been very quiet during dinner, April realized, and looked worried and tired now. In the kitchen he reached up and turned on the radio on the shelf by the sink. "Music makes the work go faster," he said. "Well now, April, how did you like cross-country skiing?"

April was about to answer when the news on the radio suddenly stopped her short. ". . . plans were announced for a huge skiing complex at Snowbird Mountain today," the announcer said smoothly. "The company plans to spend one point four million dollars. . ."

Uncle Neil's soapy hand wrenched the dial angrily and the voice died in mid-sentence. "That's enough of that!" he said angrily. April was startled. He's really worried about those developers and their money, she thought looking up at her uncle's tense face. Maybe he thinks they really *can* put Snowbird out of business and take our land!

They finished the dishes in silence, and as April crossed the living room to the loft, Danny looked up from his pile of forms and schedules. "Going to bed already?" he asked. "It's only nine o'clock, Ape."

"She's just eleven, you know," said Karen, as sweetly, April thought, as a poison dart dipped in honey.

Boy, I sure know what they mean about *Boxing* Day, April thought, as she slipped wearily under her quilt in the quiet loft a few minutes later. I feel like I've been in a boxing match with Karen all day!

CHAPTER SEVEN

What Are They Doing Here?

==========================

April woke up feeling angry. She rolled over and stared at the green blanket. The sound of deep steady breathing came from the other side. Karen was still asleep. If she says one thing, just one more nasty sarcastic thing to me today, April thought, I'm going to explode!

She got quietly out of bed and dressed quickly. Her shoulder felt normal now, and didn't hurt even when she pulled her sweatshirt over her head. She went downstairs without making a sound. There was Danny in his sleeping bag on the couch. His hair was sticking out in all directions, and he was snoring. "Sleep on, sleeping beauty," April told him and went on into the kitchen. Br-r-r! it was cold. The warmth from the living room fireplace didn't reach the kitchen and the cookstove fires had gone out before midnight.

April decided not to light the cookstove. Banging around would just wake everybody up, and she wanted to be alone. She took down the box of shredded wheat and a bowl, got some milk from the fridge, pulled a stool up to the snack bar, and sat down. Just as she was raising the first bite

56

to her lips, the kitchen door swung open. There stood Karen, in her blue velour dressing gown.

"Eating again?" Karen asked unpleasantly.

April slowly put down her spoon. "It's my breakfast," she said. "And what business is it of yours anyway?"

"Can't you wait until everybody else is eating breakfast?" Karen asked, still standing by the door. "Or do you have to sneak down early so you can get as much food as you want? So nobody sees what you eat."

"I asked you," April said, still sounding calm and reasonable, "what business it is of yours?"

"Well of course I don't care if you're getting so fat all your jeans are splitting," Karen said. "But you might think about how much it costs . . . your eating all our food . . ."

April stood up. The short fuse of her temper had been burning dangerously low ever since Karen had appeared. But that last remark was the spark that set off the explosion of anger she'd been holding back.

"At least I do something around here to earn what I eat!" she cried. "*I'm* not just a spoiled lazy brat who gets everything she wants and never lifts a finger!"

"What . . . ?" Karen started to say, shocked.

"Shut up!" said April fiercely. "I've been wanting to tell you this for a long time . . . you think that just because you can ski and are skinny, that makes you some kind of a goddess. Well, everybody around *here* might treat you like something special, but you don't seem special to me! Just a mean, selfish spoiled rotten brat . . .

that's what you seem like to me! I'm sorry I ever had to come and live with you!"

"Well, you're not the only one who wishes you'd never come!" Karen said in a low vicious voice. Both of them were trying to keep their voices down so they wouldn't wake Danny in the next room. "I wish I'd never seen you. You've ruined everything since you've come. Nothing is the same around here any more!" She turned and dashed through the door.

April stared after her, flushed with anger and shaking. It's a good thing she ran away, April thought, clenching her fists. I was just about to pull out her long blond hair by the roots! So she hates me, and wishes I didn't live here. Well, I wish I weren't here too. But how can I get away? She looked desperately around the big kitchen.

Suddenly she saw the long cross-country skis she'd used yesterday, still standing in the corner. That's how! she thought, racing over to the corner. Quickly she put on ski suit and boots and grabbed skis and poles. She was ready to go.

A cloud of frosty air curled across the floor as she opened the door; it crackled and creaked as she shut it behind her. Outside, the cold prickled the inside of her nose and felt like a tight band across her forehead. The morning light was still dim, but April could see the sun coming up, pink and gold, over the trees on the shoulder of the hill.

She stepped on the three metal prongs of the ski binding with the toe of her boot, stuck the tip of her pole in the hole in the binding and snapped it down tight the way Danny had showed her.

Then, following the twin ruts in the snow they had made yesterday, she headed for the dark opening in the wall of trees that marked the trail.

April skied hard for an hour before she stopped to rest at the bottom of a long upward slope. The anger inside was still a tight ball that urged her forward but she was also starting to feel weak with hunger, and out of breath. I don't care...she thought. I'll ski until I drop, and then...I just don't care!

Now was the time to remember how Danny had taught her to climb hills. Stomp your foot down firmly, she told herself, and keep the toes of each ski pointed outward. She was almost at the top of the hill when she suddenly felt herself slipping backwards. She fell and slid downhill in a hopeless tangle of skis and poles and legs.

April lay there, one ski wedged under a snow-covered branch, until the cold prickled her nose again. She knew it was dangerous to lie there. Deep in the trees she was sheltered from the wind, and still warm from the effort of climbing the hill; but a few minutes of lying in the snow and she would cool down, fast! But somehow she couldn't summon the energy or will to untangle her ski. She lay there in the calm woods, on a pillow of soft snow. It was so quiet, and peaceful...

Suddenly the silence was broken by the roar of an engine in the distance. A snow machine, April thought, startled and suddenly shivering. Who is it? Danny or Uncle Neil, coming to look for me? April didn't want them to find her like this! She wiggled and struggled with her pole until she got both feet loose from the ski bindings, then picked up skis and poles and plunged through the knee-deep snow up the hill.

That took ten minutes or so, and all that time the roar of the snow machine came closer and closer. April expected to see it shoot over the top of the hill at any second. But then, the sound suddenly died, as though the machine had stopped.

That's funny, April thought. If somebody's looking for me, why stop there? She plunged up the last few metres to the top, and suddenly knew why. It wasn't the neat blue machine from Snowbird Lodge down there. It was a bigger, yellow and black machine. The two riders were undoing two pairs of snowshoes from the back of the machine and strapping them on.

April gave a gasp. Even from the back and fifty metres away she recognized the smooth-fitting ski suits. Blue Suit and Beige Suit! April thought. What are they doing away out here on Snowbird Mountain's cross-country trail? The two men were in their snowshoes, and slinging large packs on their backs. April held her breath. She was afraid to move in case movement attracted their attention, but the two men seemed too busy to gaze at the scenery and soon snowshoed off up the trail to the left.

She decided to follow. What were Blue Suit and Beige Suit up to so early Monday morning — on Snowbird Mountain property? Suddenly her quarrel with Karen seemed a small thing in comparison to this threat. She was sure the ski developers had no business being there.

April snapped into her skis and hurried after the men, feeling warm again with the sudden exercise. The snowshoe trail led around the corner, up a shallow incline, and into a deep thicket of large pines. April puffed and panted up the slope, herringbone style, being careful this time not to let her skis start slipping backwards. When she reached the top of the rise she stopped.

The snowshoe tracks separated from the ski trail and wound up through the trees. April knew she couldn't follow. The snow was too deep to walk, and the pine trunks were too close together for skiing.

Just then she heard a THWACK, THWACK — the ringing sound of an axe biting into cold wood. Chopping wood? April thought, astonished. At the same moment, she caught sight of something that surprised her even more. It was a glimpse of snow-covered roof amid the trees. She was almost back to Snowbird lodge! Is that possible? April wondered, and then realized that she'd been turning to the left for a long time. That thicket of pines was the one at the base of Snowbird Mountain, to the left of the lodge.

THWACK, THWACK. The chopping sound was louder, and nearer. April wasted no more time. She pushed off down the hill, and felt her old fear return as her skis picked up speed. Don't panic, she told herself. Remember what Danny taught you. Do a half-snowplow with one ski turned in. Keep control!

Suddenly there was a loud CRACK just off to her right, and then a low groaning noise. Too late April realized that a tall pine was falling right in

61

front of her. There was no way to stop, she was going downhill too fast. WHOOSH! the great tree crashed across her path. April didn't think, she just reacted, falling backwards and sliding feet first under the massive trunk.

That quick reaction saved her. When the world stopped spinning, she found herself firmly wedged under the tree trunk, her legs stuck between the snow and the rough bark. With a shiver, April realized that if she had hit the tree a little to the right, there would have been no space under the trunk and she would have smashed into it full force.

She tried to wiggle her legs, but they were stuck tight. There's no way I'm going to get them out, April thought, fighting down panic. I'll have to yell for help — the lodge is just over there — I'll yell until someone hears me, that's all. Until someone hears me and comes and helps.

But before she could open her mouth to yell another sound broke the silence.

THWACK. The axe again. Biting into another tree. A few more strokes and there was another creak, another groan, and another huge pine came crashing down . . . this one just metres from April's head. Then she yelled!

"HEY!" she shouted with all her strength, "QUIT THAT! WILL YOU QUIT DROPPING TREES ON MY HEAD!"

The axe stopped. They had heard. "Who's there?" came a deep voice that April recognized.

"I'M STUCK UNDER YOUR STUPID TREE!" April bellowed at the top of her lungs, furious as well as scared. "COME AND GET ME OUT!"

There was a long moment of silence, during which April felt the cold come creeping through her ski suit. She wondered if the two men had gone back to their snow machine. They had no business cutting down Snowbird Mountain trees and they were probably the kind of men who would leave a person stuck under a tree to save their own hides, she thought bitterly. Her legs felt pinched and cramped; she would soon lose feeling in them.

"Well, well, well, if it isn't our little waitress from the lodge," she suddenly heard behind her. Squinting up, she saw the smooth-shaven, tanned face of Blue Suit gazing down at her. The two men had snowshoed very silently up behind her.

"Get me out of here!" April said, furiously.

"Just a matter of releasing her binding and pulling her back out of her skis, I should think," offered Beige Suit. April noticed for the first time that he spoke with a slight British accent. Blue Suit, she thought, might be American.

"What are you doing, cutting down trees on Snowbird Mountain property, and letting them fall across the ski trail?" April demanded, as Blue Suit climbed over the tree trunk to reach her binding release.

"Oh, we're just cutting some lot marker stakes. You seem to be a little upset," commented Blue Suit with a too-wide smile. "Naturally, we didn't think there'd *be* anybody skiing. After all, it has been very cold, hasn't it?"

"That doesn't explain why you're trespassing on private property and chopping down private pine trees!" April sputtered. She had the awful feeling she was way out of her depth with these two smoothies.

"Oh ho! So you think this property belongs to your family, do you?" laughed Beige Suit, putting a large gloved hand under April's shoulder and starting to pull.

"What do you mean. . . I think? Of course it . . . OW!" April protested. "Can you pull on my other shoulder? That one's just been separated!"

"We are prone to accidents, aren't we, dear?" said Beige Suit, maddeningly amused. He reached under the other armpit and slowly dragged April out from under the tree.

Shaking with fury, cold and indignant, she struggled to her feet. She hated, loathed and detested being called 'dear'! And what did they mean acting so know-it-all and righteous, when they were so obviously in the wrong?

The important thing now was to get back to the lodge and get help. April threw her skis over the tree trunk, climbed over herself and snapped her feet into the bindings.

"Are you sure you're all right?" called the man with the English accent, but April skied away without a backward glance.

The tow was humming when April, puffing and exhausted, skied out of the woods. Uncle Neil must be in the shack, April thought, and pushed the last few strides towards it. But as she pushed through the line of skiers waiting to go up the tow, she saw that it was Danny running the tow.

The lodge door opened and Uncle Neil came out. But he wasn't heading for the tow, he was going around the lodge to the parking lot.

"Uncle Neil!" she cried. "Wait!"

Her uncle turned and shielded his eyes from the sun as she ran across the snow towards him.

"Uncle Neil, those two men," April panted, "the ones from the development company... they're back in the woods cutting our trees! They nearly brained me with one!"

Uncle Neil looked startled and then stern. "Nora has been worried about you," he said. "You'd better go inside and let her know you're back. I have to get to town." He turned to go.

"But Uncle Neil..." April said urgently. What was wrong with her uncle? Blue Suit and Beige Suit would be getting away if he didn't hurry!

He patted her awkwardly on the shoulder, not looking at her. "Please don't tell your aunt...or the others...that you saw them," he said. "There's nothing we can do about it now."

April tried not to let her mouth fall open in astonishment. "But..." she started to protest.

Uncle Neil shook his head wearily. "I'm late for an appointment at the bank," he said. "We can talk later."

April stared as he turned away and climbed into the truck. What did he mean, "There's nothing we can do about it?" People couldn't just trespass on your property and cut down your trees! Then April seemed to hear Blue Suit's nasty laughter ringing in her ears. What was it he had said? "So you think this land belongs to your family?" A terrible suspicion began to grow in April's mind as she watched her uncle's truck spin away down Snowbird Mountain Road. She turned to walk back to the lodge. There were already half a dozen cars in the parking lot, and a good sprinkling of skiers on the hill. Everything looked normal at Snowbird—but something was very wrong.

All morning April waited for Uncle Neil to return from the bank, but when he finally arrived at one, he changed his clothes and went straight to work. Aunt Nora had not given April a big lecture about going skiing without telling anyone; she'd been too busy. They were all too busy with a lodge full of skiers needing food, and tow tickets, and rental equipment.

Only Danny was his usual cheerful self and April almost poured out her troubles to him when he came in for his usual three hot dogs and two litres of ketchup.

"I hear you were out on the trail this morning!" he grinned at her. "How was it?"

"Good," April lied. "I saw those two guys . . ."

"Oh really?" Danny said, getting his mouth around his bulging hotdog. "What were they doing? Trying to figure out where to put their international airport?"

"That's the thing," April said, leaning over the counter. "I don't know what they were doing! They had a snow machine."

"Maybe they were planning their two million dollar health spa . . . or a beauty shop . . ." Danny went on, laughing.

"Get serious!" April said. "This is important."

"I know . . ." Danny started to say, but just then a couple of guys he knew from high school came in and their conversation ended.

66

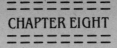
The First Challenge

"If only we didn't have to go back to school!" Karen groaned, next Monday morning at breakfast. "All that perfect snow out there, and I have to be stuck in school. The dumb bus doesn't get us out here until five, and by that time, it's dark!"

Charming, April thought, studying her cousin's stormy face. As soon as Karen gets off her skis, her personality self-destructs.

"I'm going to lose all my momentum!" Karen went on, "My legs will stiffen up before the weekend. If only I could get a couple of runs after school!"

"I suppose I could come into town and pick you up early," Uncle Neil said slowly. "What time is your last class?"

Once again April was amazed at how much her aunt and uncle seemed ready to sacrifice for Karen's skiing. It was almost a thirty-kilometre drive on snowy roads to the high school, and another thirty back.

"I have geography last period," groaned Karen. "I'm not done until three-thirty. Can't I just miss geography until after the first Challenge Cup? That way Dad could pick me up a little after two."

"You know the school rules on missing classes," Aunt Nora said. "You'll fail any test you miss and have to write your final exam in June."

"It's not fair!" cried Karen.

"Maybe it's not fair but it's a fact," said her mother firmly. "I think it's up to you, Karen. If you can make up your work, and don't mind writing that exam . . ."

Karen pushed her plate of pancakes aside and sat with her chin on her hands. April felt almost sorry for her cousin. Karen had to make decisions like this all the time; exams or skiing, friends or skiing, fun or skiing!

"What about you, April?" asked Uncle Neil. "Could you be ready to leave school early, if I came in to pick you girls up?"

Karen's pale face flushed an angry red. "It's got nothing to do with April!" she shouted. April stopped her forkful of pancake halfway to her lips. That's what you get for feeling sorry for *Karen*, she thought. Prepare for battle!

"I like the bus," April said quickly, getting up and taking her plate to the sink. "I don't want a ride."

"But you should be training too," Aunt Nora said, "now that your shoulder is better." She flashed a critical look at April's expanding waistline and sagging posture.

"I don't *mind* the bus . . ." April started to say again. Why didn't anybody listen to her?

"Training! Ha! That's a good one!" Karen exploded. "I'd like to see you train her for anything besides the eating Olympics!"

"Karen!" cried Aunt Nora in a shocked voice.

"Well, it's true. Just look at her! You're going to waste time trying to teach that *blob* how to ski?"

April saw red. Suddenly she felt all the Martineau spirit well up inside her. Her uncle and aunt were staring at their daughter as though they had never seen this side of her before.

"You're right, Aunt Nora," she said calmly. But her fingers were crossed tight behind her back against the terrible lie she was about to tell. "I'm dying to get back up on Snowbird Mountain again." The two girls faced each other, staring. Karen scarlet and white, April deadly calm, with blazing dark eyes.

"Well," said Aunt Nora at last. "Then that's settled. Neil or I will come in and pick you both up at two-fifteen."

And so it was decided. At ten to seven the two girls were on the dark road leading to the highway. Karen, as always, jogged the snow-packed road, using it as part of her training program. April usually poked along, enjoying the whole white world lightening with the dawn. This morning she decided to hurry, not run exactly, but just walk fast. It helped her hurrying thoughts.

She felt warm inside with the triumph of standing up to Karen. And scared stiff of her promise to try downhill skiing again. And worried about Blue Suit and Beige Suit. Why hadn't they come back? And why had Uncle Neil let them tramp all over Snowbird and never explain why? Aunt Nora had put on a brave front saying that they would never sell, but Uncle Neil looked crushed and defeated these days, even though business had been so good! She wished he would come right out in the open and say what was bothering him, the way her dad always had.

April watched the slim figure of her cousin jogging ahead in the rosy dawn light. If what I think is true, there won't be any more racing or champions, April thought. There won't be any more Snowbird Mountain. April remembered what it felt like to have your whole world suddenly fall apart. No matter how spoiled and miserable her cousin was, she didn't deserve that!

All week April trained hard, starting by walking a few metres up the beginner's hill and skiing down. It was hard work, but it strengthened her legs. By the end of the week she was going up the tow and coming down the beginner's slope with confidence again. She still felt sick at the thought of going to the top.

"That was a good run!" called Uncle Neil, as she skied up to him.

"Bah! Good for the baby hill!" April heard Karen mutter as she slid onto the tow bar beside her. Karen was taking the tow to the top, where Aunt Nora was coaching her for the Challenge Cup.

"Just a couple more runs," Uncle Neil warned. "It's getting dark."

"Can't you come up and tell me how I'm doing, Dad?" Karen begged. "My turns still don't feel right."

"I'm helping April," Uncle Neil said. "You'll do fine."

Karen threw April a look of utter scorn as they

sailed off up the tow. "Here's your stop," she said, as they reached the top of the beginner's hill. "Have fun."

April watched her go up the rest of the hill, lounging back on the bar, not even holding on, as if she'd been born on a ski tow. I'll show her, April thought fiercely, shoving off with her ski poles, oh boy, will I!

That night, as every night, Uncle Neil prepared Karen for the race with lectures on slalom skiing, movies that he'd taken of races, and diagrams of race courses, drawn on an old chalkboard in the living room. April, struggling with her homework by the fireplace, learned a lot by just listening.

"Remember," Uncle Neil said, "the course won't be set until the day of the race. But Friday, I want you to go over that hill so often you know it like the back of your hand. You've got to know where every bump is, every icy patch, every speck of exposed gravel. Then Saturday, when the flags go up, stay on the hill as much as you can. It's against the rules to ski through the course, but run it *mentally*, taking into account what you know about the hill."

Uncle Neil would not be there. Someone would have to stay at Snowbird and run the weekend ski school. Aunt Nora would act as coach to Karen and Danny.

"I'd like you to go to Timmins with them," Uncle Neil said to April.

April looked up from her books in surprise.

"We always need another hand at a race," Uncle Neil went on. "Someone to help with

71

equipment and make sure our racers' times are recorded properly."

"And whether you're needed or not," Aunt Nora smiled at April, "you've earned it with all those hours in the snack bar. It's given Karen a lot more training time than she would have had."

Karen stared steadfastly at the race diagram and didn't look at them. I know what she's thinking, April sighed. Why do I have to tag along and ruin everything. But Aunt Nora's right — I have earned this trip, and I'm going! Besides, it will put off skiing from the top of Snowbird for one more week!

The next Friday morning, they were sitting in a pancake house in Timmins, and April was trying to decide between buttermilk and strawberry crêpes.

"How will we get out to Kam?" Karen asked. They'd taken the bus to the centre of Timmins, but the ski hill was still fifteen kilometres away.

"Taxi," Aunt Nora answered, not looking up.

"That's going to cost a fortune!" Danny said.

"I know," said Aunt Nora. "It's expensive getting to races."

Just then a tall slim man in ski clothes came striding up to the table, smiling and holding out his hand to Aunt Nora. He had reddish hair and freckles, and his face was creased with laugh lines.

"Nora Hearst!"

"Hello! It's John Bukowski, isn't it?" smiled Aunt Nora. At the name *Bukowski*, April saw Karen's head shoot up, and a flush of excitement brushed her cheeks. Who is he? April wondered.

"Are you here for the Challenge Cup?" The young man's eyes swept over the three of them, and then went back to gazing at Aunt Nora with a look of almost adoration.

"Of course we are," Aunt Nora said. "These are our young racers, my daughter Karen and our friend Danny. And my niece, April Martineau; she's just learning to ski."

"Your niece? Yes, she has your eyes," the young man said. "Well, young lady, with a coach like Nora Hearst, you'll be racing in no time!"

"But I haven't introduced *you*," laughed Aunt Nora. "Kids, this is John Bukowski, assistant coach for the Northern Divisional Ski Team."

"And your mother's fan," John looked at Karen, who flushed even more. "I was your age, and just starting to race, when she was on the Olympic Team. She was the greatest!" He grinned. "Still is, of course."

So that's why he looks as though he'd like Aunt Nora's autograph, thought April. It was sometimes hard to remember that Aunt Nora had been a famous skier. She never talks about it or makes a big deal of it, April thought. Not like some people!

"I'm here to look out for skiers for my training squad," John said, "and of course hopefuls for the divisional team next year." His eyes twinkled as he looked at Karen and Danny's tense faces. There was no need to ask if they were hoping to get on the team. Their faces said it all.

"Do you have your car?" John asked. "I'd be glad to give you all a lift out to the hill in the team van, if you'd like."

April saw Karen and Danny exchange looks of

pure bliss. Knowing the assistant coach—riding in the official team van—they were in heaven!

The Kamiskotia Ski Hill looked like a wart on the flat tree-covered land that stretched north from Timmins. As they swung into the 'SKI KAM' road, April saw an old, deserted fire tower on top of the hill.

"Snowbird's twice as high," April said to her aunt, as they unloaded skis from the back of the van.

"I keep telling you, pet, the size of the hill hasn't much to do with producing champions," laughed Aunt Nora. "Some of the best Canadian skiers have come from Timmins."

"Mother!" cried Karen, appearing around the side of the van. "Isn't John wonderful? You didn't tell me he was a *friend*! He's going to give Danny and me special coaching today."

"He'd do that anyway," Aunt Nora said, handing Karen her boot bag. "That's his job. The better skier you are, the more attention you'll get from him. He's in the business of developing champions."

Karen looked scared and pleased at the same time, as she planted a quick kiss on her mother's cheek and dashed off after Danny and John Bukowski, who were deep in conversation as they headed for the chalet.

"It's all up to them now," sighed Aunt Nora as she watched Karen go. "You and I, April, are just the donkeys on this expedition. I hope you don't mind being sent here and there for this and that." She slammed the back doors of the van, and heavily laden, they started across the parking lot.

"Of course I don't mind," April said quickly. "It's all for Snowbird Mountain, isn't it?"

Aunt Nora's eyes were suddenly full of a look April had never seen before. "I'm glad you feel that way," Aunt Nora said. "You've become very important at Snowbird, you know." She put her arm, boot bag and all, around April's shoulders and gave her a big hug. April suddenly felt very warm, despite the cold snowy day. Now if Karen could only feel that way.

It was a day, as Aunt Nora said, of being sent all over the place for all kinds of things — files to sharpen ski edges, spare parts for ski poles, and hamburgers for lunch!

The chalet at Kam was full of stomping, determined young skiers, comparing equipment, comparing run times. April couldn't help envying their close feeling of being part of a group. They had known each other for a long time and shared a common goal: to make the Canadian Ski Team. Even though the goal was intensely serious, there was a lot of laughing and kidding around. A big, bright fire burned in the chalet's woodstove, and photographs of Kam's famous skiers crowded the walls.

A wide deck stretched the length of the chalet, and from there April watched the skiers snaking down the Chalet Run directly in front of her. Once in a while she spotted Danny or Karen, learning the hill, as Uncle Neil had taught them.

"I've hit every mogul from every angle," puffed Danny when they stopped for a break. "I could ski it in my sleep!"

"It's all rocky at the top," Karen frowned. "I'm

carving up my skis something terrible up there."

Aunt Nora looked concerned. Scratched skis were a serious problem in racing, as any defect in the sliding surface could cost precious fractions of seconds. "Too bad we didn't bring old skis for practice," she said.

"These *are* old skis," Karen said, running her hand-down the metal edges of her slalom skis. "You should see some of the new ones the kids have. They make these look like planks."

"I know," Aunt Nora agreed. "We hoped you'd have new equipment this year . . ." She paused, looking up at Karen.

"If I can just do well in these Challenge Cup races," Karen said, "then the suppliers will be begging me to wear their skis. That's how it works, isn't it?"

Aunt Nora put up a warning hand. "That's how it works, maybe, but you've got a long way to go. How about a few more runs before the tow closes? Try to keep off the worst parts of the hill. You know it well enough by now."

Danny and Karen stood up to go. Then a frown creased Danny's face. "There's the guy I have to beat," he said, pointing to a tall boy in a brown ski suit flying towards the tow line-up. "That's Todd Hartford from Sudbury."

"I remember him from last year," Aunt Nora nodded. "He's good."

"He's been beating me since we were ten," said Danny. "And he's grown eight centimetres since last year."

"He's a show-off!" Karen said, watching Todd almost careen into the line of waiting skiers. "And

I think your size is better for racing," she added loyally.

Danny grinned at April. His grin said clearly, "See she's not so bad," and April smiled back. She had to agree, the best thing about her cousin's rotten personality was her loyalty to Danny.

When the tow closed in another hour, the young skiers tromped wearily into the chalet, gratefully soaking up its warmth as they shed stiff boots and gloves. The talk was all of racing.

"John says you lose time if you clip the pole," Karen said to her mother as she banged her left foot to loosen the boot. "But the kids all do it. They say it gives them the fastest line for the next gate if you go close."

"Close, but not touching," Aunt Nora said, snapping Karen's boots together in their rack. "Every time you hit a pole, you slow down, just a fraction."

Just then, the boy Danny had identified as Todd Hartford swaggered up to their table. His eyes flicked over April without recognition, looked hard at Danny, and settled on Karen with a look half of embarrassment and half admiration.

"Guess we'll see you back at the Senator," he said. The Senator was the biggest and one of the fanciest hotels in Timmins.

"Nope," Danny said cheerfully. "We're not staying there."

"No?" asked Todd in surprise. "All the kids are staying there. Why don't you come over? There's going to be a party."

"The coach says no parties," smiled Aunt Nora, and Todd looked at the small slender woman in surprise. There was just a hint of boldness in his voice as he asked, "Your coach?"

"That's correct," Danny said, and April could see that he was struggling to control his temper. Karen looked embarrassed. Danny finished zipping his boot bag with a jerk. "See you on the hill tomorrow."

"Sure!" Todd shrugged, and with a last smile at Karen he clomped away in his ski boots. "May the best man win!"

Just then they heard the cheerful voice of John Bukowski behind them. "Can I offer your gang a lift back to our motel?" April saw Todd stop in mid-stride and whip around as if he couldn't believe his ears. The assistant coach was smiling at Aunt Nora.

Suddenly, staying at the WigMac seemed the best choice anyone could have made. Leaving Todd standing with his mouth open, Karen, Danny and April quickly gathered their gear and followed John and Aunt Nora out to the van.

Later, after an enormous steak and pie dinner, Danny and Karen worked on the surfaces of the skis with a kofix candle, dripping melted plastic into the scratches and smoothing it with a scraper. April sat cross-legged beside them, handing them whatever they needed from the waxing kit.

"Feel ready for tomorrow?" Aunt Nora asked.

"Ready!" Danny said firmly, and April knew he was thinking about Todd Hartford and how much he'd like to beat him.

"We've just got to win!" said Karen, turning her ski to the light to check that it was perfectly smooth. The narrow beam of light from the motel's reading lamp heightened the shadows under her cheekbones and made her look, April thought, like a proud northern princess.

"Hey, Ape," said Danny, interrupting her thoughts, "how did you like your first day at a race?"

"I . . . it was . . . " April started, trying to put her feelings into words.

"You can't really expect her to get much out of it," Karen said lightly. "She's not part of it."

April felt the smile fading from her face. Karen had found the five most hurtful words in the world to say. I *did* feel part of it; I *was* part of it until just now, April thought.

CHAPTER NINE

A Challenge Met

====================================

The next two days passed like a dream for April. She felt herself caught up in a world of speed and excitement. Full of the noises of the loudspeaker: "They're in the hair-pin." "They're in the last gate." "Danny Antoniazzi of Snowbird Mountain, with a time of 29.30 seconds..." And full of the sight of skiers: speeding down between two sets of red-flagged poles, skiing unbelievably fast, unbelievably close to the poles... and some falling...

The falls were terrible. Each time April saw a young racer careening down the hill, head over heels, she relived the nightmare of her own fall. When skiers were brought down on the ski patrol sleds with injured arms or legs, she wondered how any of the others had the courage to go up there again.

Her heart pounded with suspense each time Danny or Karen was one of the figures in the starting gate. She ached with tension, waiting for the split second their thigh touched the starting wand and activated the radio-controlled timer's clock.

By Saturday night, Karen's name was second on the chalkboard list, with a time of 32.75 seconds. Danny was fourth among the boys and Todd Hartford was on top.

Sunday came, as bright and promising as its name, and the finals! April felt she must be as nervous as Danny, fiercely filing his edges, or Karen, polishing her wax job to perfection. They both seemed calm, even remote. It was April who had butterflies flip-flopping in her stomach.

Kamiskotia Ski Club was a sea of unfamiliar faces. Parents, friends, coaches and curious spectators turned up for the finals of the Challenge Cup on this beautiful winter day. April saw people point at Karen's name on the board, and heard them whisper, "Who is Karen Hearst? Where is she from?" as if someone from a little out-of-the-way club like Snowbird had no right to challenge the big ski hills like Sault Ste. Marie and Sudbury. The other top skiers had a horde of well-dressed supporters hovering around them. Karen and Danny had only Aunt Nora and herself.

But by three o'clock when the semi-final races were completed, there were only four names left on the board: Karen Hearst of Snowbird skiing against Tina Kallonen of the Sault, and Danny Antoniazzi against Todd Hartford in the final heat.

Now the watchers on the deck were full of Snowbird Mountain stories; how it was one of the best hills in Northern Ontario, how Aunt Nora and Uncle Neil had once been champions. People

started to remember, and there was a new excitement born, as if *they* had discovered or created Snowbird Mountain themselves!

April hugged herself with excitement. She didn't think she would be able to breathe through the last race. The shadows on the hill were growing long. The tiny figures at the top seemed so far away, the waiting so unbearable.

And suddenly they were moving. First Karen and then Tina Kallonen, knees bending, bodies turning, skis carving the same perfect track through the poles. As Tina rocketed through the last gate, a great cheer for both girls went up from the crowd, and then came the long, agonizing moment of complete silence, waiting for the judge's announcement. April held her breath . . .

"Karen Hearst, the winner, with a time of 31.08 seconds." An incredible time. Both girls had bested any time for that race by more than a full second. Another cheer rose, this time all for Karen. April felt tears of joy pricking behind her eyes as she ran to help Karen out of her skis, but Karen was staying in them. "I'm going to the top to watch Danny," she called back to April.

If only I could be there too! April thought, returning to her place on the deck. Just to wish him luck! She could see Karen already on the tow, alone on the T-bar, arms relaxed, back in her element. And she isn't like the other girls who win the heats, April thought—the way they strut around and giggle and toss their heads. She isn't really interested in all the glory. Racing means something else to her and Danny. Something I don't understand yet.

The boys' race lacked the beautiful, soaring rhythm of the girls'. Todd Hartford attacked the poles as though they were personal enemies, striking each one as he skied dangerously close. Danny's turns were carved in fierce sprays of snow. April found herself praying: Please God, don't let him fall!

But it was Todd who fell, hitting the tricky hairpin gate at the wrong angle, trying to correct too late, throwing his body off balance and tumbling, crashing, skidding down the hill. The race was over, and Danny had won! April saw him race over to make sure his rival was all right, and a cheer went up as he helped Todd to his feet.

It's all over! April thought. Two white lines were being drawn under Danny's and Karen's names. Joy rushed through April like an electric current. It's over, and Snowbird had won!

Standing looking up at the chalkboard, April suddenly caught sight of a familiar blue ski suit and a smooth, tanned neck. Oh no! not Blue Suit, she thought, but his tall, super-groomed figure was unmistakable.

Then he turned, with his greasy smile, and caught Aunt Nora's eye. "Congratulations, Mrs. Hearst," he purred, pointing to the board. "Your skiers have done well!"

"You bet!" said Aunt Nora, obviously bristling at the sight of him. "I told you we trained champions at Snowbird."

"And that's exactly what we would like to do."

"Then you'll have to go find your own hill!" Aunt Nora said sharply. "Excuse me." She rushed away to meet Karen and Danny.

April hated the sneaky, 'I know something you don't know' look on Blue Suit's face as he watched Aunt Nora run down the deck steps and catch Karen in her arms. Like he was some kind of all-powerful god who could control our lives with a snap of his fingers, April thought. She watched him stroll arrogantly away towards the bar.

A few minutes later, at the awards ceremony, April saw him again. He was standing, a head taller than anyone else, at the back of the crowd of friends and photographers. Karen and Danny were on the top step of the winner's stand, each holding one racing ski; on the lower steps were Todd Hartford and Tina Kallonen, and the third place winners. As the gold medals were draped around Danny and Karen's necks, flashbulbs popped and the crowd applauded. But not Blue Suit. April saw him reach in his ski jacket pocket for a notepad and write something down.

Aunt Nora was coming towards her now, her arms linked with her two winners, and her face shining like a Christmas tree. She's forgotten all about Blue Suit and the danger he represents, April thought desperately. As far as Aunt Nora's concerned, 'Not for Sale' means 'Not for Sale', and that's all there is to it. But she didn't see them marking their lots right beside the lodge, and she mustn't have noticed how awful Uncle Neil's been looking lately. I wish I could tell her!

But now was definitely *not* the time. John Bukowski, grinning from ear to ear, was congratulating Aunt Nora. "Well!" he said. "Well!"

"John Bukowski, if you say *one* thing about these two following in my footsteps, I'll kick you down Kam's Bunny Patch!" Aunt Nora said sternly. "They did it themselves, all of it!"

"Of course, naturally, all right!" John laughed, his handsome face crinkling up. "But I'd say this calls for a celebration. What do you all say to steak and chocolate sundaes at the WigMac?"

As they gathered their skis and equipment and headed for the van, April caught a last glimpse of Blue Suit. Everyone else was too happy and excited to notice him, striding away towards the parking lot.

The return to Snowbird Mountain was a triumphant one. Uncle Neil hung Danny's and Karen's gold medals on the brick shelf above the fireplace and toasted them in delicious hot whipped chocolate he'd made especially for the homecoming.

"Here's to our winners!" he said. "You've put Snowbird Mountain back on the map!" April, remembering all the talk that had buzzed around Karen and Danny, thought her uncle was right. Even Blue Suit had been impressed.

"I'll drink to that," Aunt Nora agreed, a wide smile lighting up her face. "Do you remember John Bukowski, Neil? He's the Divisional assistant coach now. He was very pleased with both of them."

"I'm not surprised," Uncle Neil grinned. He reached behind him for an album from the bookcase, flipped it open and held it out so April, Karen and Danny could see. "That's John," he said. "I'll never forget him. Everywhere we went, there was this little red-headed kid, hero-worshipping Nora!"

April saw a picture of a slim young woman in a ski suit, a tall man with his arm around her, and a boy, holding a pair of skis. At first she thought the woman must be Karen, Aunt Nora looked so young! And John Bukowski was shorter than she was.

"I didn't recognize him at first," Aunt Nora laughed. "He's grown about a metre!"

April pointed to another picture of a young man with skis. "Who's that?" she asked, curiously.

Aunt Nora looked up and her brown eyes were warm and full of pity. "That's your dad," she said softly.

"Oh!" said April staring at the picture. He looked so different, so young without his beard; it seemed so funny to see him there, when he was . . . gone.

Karen's mind was on the future, not the past. "John's going to help me," she said. "He's a terrific coach, Dad. He says when you go into a race, just to forget technique, and concentrate on winning."

"All very well — if you have your technique," Uncle Neil reminded her.

The talk swirled on, about racing, and equipment, and timing. . . April held the open album on her lap and watched the fire, thinking that you could no more catch and hold the past than one of those dancing flames. John Bukowski was no more a little boy, he had turned into a man. And Aunt Nora was a businesswoman, and a mother; and her father was . . . dead. It hurt to think that word. April closed the book and curled up tight in the blue velvet chair. She hardly noticed when Danny got up to leave.

After he'd gone, Aunt Nora reached over and took April's hand. "Now that that race is behind us, we'll have to get you up to the top of Snowbird," she smiled. "Are you ready to give it a try?"

April snapped out of her dream world and suddenly sat up straight. "The top. . . ?" she said, and then caught Karen's challenging look. Maybe Karen will accept me if I get to be a really good skier, April thought, thinking of how close her cousin was to Danny. And what have I got to lose except a couple of broken legs? "Sure," she told her aunt, "any time." She sounded a lot braver than she felt.

"Good," said Aunt Nora, giving her hand a pat. "Tomorrow."

CHAPTER TEN

From the Top Again

================================

The T-bar came around behind April and her aunt and caught them at the tops of their thighs. April leaned gently against it as it started to lift, concentrating on keeping her skis straight in the track, and tried not to think they were going to the top! But as they passed the path through the pines that led to the beginner's hill, the tow gave a sudden hitch and lurch, as though preparing itself for the *big* climb ahead. Well, thought April, here I go!

Straight up 'The Exterminator' they climbed. In summer, this was a sheer drop of rock; in winter, packed with snow, it was the last thirty metres of the tow path. April could simply not imagine anyone skiing down the vertical runs to the right and left of the tow. She was beginning to feel the icy fear, clawing at her stomach, weakening her grip on the tow bar.

"Off. . . Now!" shouted Aunt Nora, as they inched up the last metre. April let go of the bar and let the 'T' slide out from under her. It swayed gently in the air above them.

Aunt Nora skied to the top of the run, and stopped, waiting for April to catch up. Her legs feeling like rubber, April followed. The setting sun at the top of Snowbird Mountain lit her aunt's face softly and the wind blew a strand of loose hair across her forehead. She suddenly looked a lot like the girl in the photograph album.

"This is the time to talk about being afraid," Aunt Nora said, "when you have to face it." April tried desperately not to look at the wonderful view from the top, the distant purple and gold sky, the black forest so far below . . .

"You seem to ski without fear on the beginner's hill . . ."

April nodded, wishing she were on the beginner's hill right now. Her legs were turning to jello!

"So, I think you're afraid of heights, not skiing," Aunt Nora said. "Up here, you feel very high — but actually you're not even one centimetre off the ground. You're just as firmly on the ground as you are in front of the lodge. Think about it."

April thought. It was true, but it didn't take away the cold fist of fear inside her. In a moment she would be flying down that awful hill.

"And don't look at the whole hill," Aunt Nora went on. "Look at the first few metres, over to that little spruce on the right of the run, and see, the ground's almost flat between here and there."

April forced herself to look. Pretty flat . . . cute tree . . . but so what? There was still the rest of the hill.

Aunt Nora suddenly shoved off and skied very slowly, over to the spruce tree.

"Now *you* do that," she called.

They were all alone up there. There was no one to see her if she fell. April jerked her eyes away from the terrible cold emptiness below them and shoved off across the hill.

"Good!" cried Aunt Nora, as April snowplowed to a stop almost on top of the tree. "Now, point your skis in the opposite direction and follow me over to that little mogul over there. Keep your eyes on me and follow my trail exactly." Once again she skied very slowly across the hill. April, watching to see that her skis stayed in her aunt's tracks, followed.

"Keep your weight on your downhill ski!" Aunt Nora called. "Rotate your left shoulder a little downhill. That's good . . . that's fine!" April reached her, *and* passed her, and slid helplessly into the deep snow at the side of the trail.

"To put on the brakes," said Aunt Nora, helping her dig out of the snow and get turned around, "try turning your skis uphill. Brakes are handy . . . no, don't look down!"

April gave a shudder as she realized that once more she was at the lip of the 'nosedive'. Ice-blue and terrible, the ground fell away from them in one great swoop of snow.

"I . . . can't . . . " she stammered.

"Sure you can," said Aunt Nora matter-of-factly. She shoved off and skied casually across the very lip of the nosedive, just as if it weren't there.

April suddenly felt very alone. The mountain and the sky didn't care if she made it down in one piece. The last rays of sun had left the snow and the cold clamped down. "I can't," said April again

91

but no one heard her. Aunt Nora waited, a small red figure on the other side of the run. "You have to!" whispered another voice inside. "Trust Aunt Nora..."

"I CAN'T!" whispered April.

"Then you're just a big blob, like Karen said..."

It was the thought of her big-shot, smart alek, know-it-all cousin that gave April the final shove she needed. Rigid with fear, she let herself slide forward, slowly, centimetre by centimetre, across the face of the hill. Eyes fixed on the twin shadows of her aunt's tracks, legs aching, hands tightly clutching her poles, she edged her way across the top of the nosedive.

"There!" smiled Aunt Nora, as April came tremblingly to a stop next to her. "Easy, wasn't it?"

Easy?

"You'll never lose control on a hill again," said Aunt Nora firmly. "You'll fall lots—as long as you ski—but never again because you got scared and went into free fall."

April suddenly looked up at her aunt's smiling face. It was true. It *was* pretty easy after all—keep your skis pointed up the hill, put your weight on the top ski—rotate your shoulder.

"We'd better see if we can get down before dark," grinned Aunt Nora. "If you're ready for the rest."

"I'm ready!" cried April, taking a looser grip on the poles.

Back and forth across the hill, they wove their way down. April concentrated fiercely on keeping

in her aunt's tracks. She was surprised when suddenly they swept out on the beginner's hill and the lights of the lodge twinkled below them.

"Okay," called Aunt Nora. "You're on your own!"

Joyously, April shoved off with her poles. Slide forward, bend the knees, down, extend, turn. She felt as though she were flying, free, and yet in control. It was over too fast, and she was sliding over the last few metres of snow, up to the door of the lodge.

April stopped, panting, and looked back and up. The last red rays of the sun just touched the tip of the highest tow tower. A pair of ravens soared over the pines. I did it! April suddenly thought, shaking with happiness. Snowbird Mountain no longer looked strange and terrible, but like an old friend.

We can't lose you to those ski developers, she thought fiercely. We can't! You're ours!

April couldn't wait until Saturday when Danny came. She waited until he came down the hill and then hurried up to him at the tow.

"Can I go up with you?"

Danny looked over his shoulder in surprise. "Yeah! Sure! Why not?" Danny grinned. "Want to get off here?" he asked as they approached the beginner's hill.

"No," said April, "do you?"

"Oh, no. I just thought . . . never mind." He seemed puzzled. "Have you been taking lessons again, Ape? I mean, I thought . . ."

"Which run do you want to take?" April asked blithely, ignoring his confusion.

"Well...uh..."

"How about the 'Exterminator'?"

"The Ex...!" Danny's voice cracked in surprise.

"But please take it slow, Danny," April asked. "I wouldn't want to get too far behind."

"You go first," Danny insisted. "I'll be right behind you all the way."

"Okay," agreed April breezily, and shoved off.

She slipped gracefully down the hill, determined to make a perfect run. She'd been working very hard on her turns all week, and the work had paid off. Now, when she shifted her weight, her skis came obediently and smoothly around, making a zig-zag path down the first two hundred metres of the hill. She stopped at the bottom of the fearsome 'Nosedive' and waited, laughing, for Danny to catch up.

When he did he attacked. Threw snow, shoved her, skis and all, into a snowbank and called her every name he could think of in French, English and Italian.

"I guess that means I'm pretty good, eh?" April laughed.

"Pretty *good*! What happened? At Christmas you were so scared!"

"Oh, just Aunt Nora's teaching," April said, wiping the snow off her face, "and my natural athletic talent, of course."

"Oh no!" groaned Danny. "Now I've got two know-it-all girls to put up with!"

"And speaking of know-it-alls, here she comes," muttered April, as Karen's light blue suit flashed towards them down the hill.

They waited for Karen to stop and talk, but she flew by in a tight racing crouch, not even glancing in their direction.

"Just reminding me that I'd better get back to work," Danny said. A worried frown crossed his forehead. "I really don't have much of a chance at the next Challenge Cup race with the little skiing I've had!"

"I know you'll win," April said loyally.

Danny shrugged. "We can only try. In the meantime, *you* keep up the good work! You'll be racing with us soon."

He pushed off down the 'Exterminator' and April followed. She soon realized it would be dangerous to try to keep up with Danny. He'd forgotten what a slow turn was, if he'd ever known. April watched him hurtle out of sight.

I'll never be a racer, she thought. But it would be fun to go fast like that!

At the bottom of the hill she had a sudden impulse, and went to the tow shack to see her Uncle Neil. The tow was busy, fully loaded with afternoon skiers.

"Can I help, Uncle Neil?" she asked, knowing that this was usually Danny's duty. It wasn't a hard job, just making sure that the T-bars came straight out of the shack, handing them to the skiers, and helping little kids or novices get on. She'd watched many times by now, and was sure she could do it.

"Thanks, April. But you're pretty small for the job," Uncle Neil said, looking down at her. "We can't afford a break in the line just now. One person falling off the tow trips the safety switch and the whole towline grinds to a halt. Skiers who've paid for a tow ticket hate to be kept waiting at the bottom, or worse, stuck halfway up!" He sighed, looking at the old machinery. "Unfortunately, it happens here all too often!" He steadied the T-bar for the next customers.

"Your aunt might like some help in the Snack Bar, though," Uncle Neil smiled. "And thanks again for the offer."

I'll be glad when I'm older and taller, April thought, then I can...She suddenly stopped short. Getting on the next T-bar were Blue Suit and Beige Suit!

"Uncle Neil," she cried, as they glided away up the hill, "what are they doing here?" Her uncle was watching Blue Suit and Beige Suit anxiously, his eyebrows drawn together in a tight frown.

"Why they're, uh...skiing I guess," Uncle Neil said weakly. He looked as surprised as April to see them and his usually calm face was twisted with concern.

"But, Uncle Neil, this is a private ski hill...I mean it's *ours*, isn't it? We don't have to let them ski here?" April was suddenly stammering. What if Snowbird didn't belong to them any longer? She hated the look on Uncle Neil's face!

"It's all right, April," he said quietly. "Maybe you should go in and help your aunt." Just then, there was a terrible clashing and churning of gears. The tow was jammed and the long line of skiers suddenly stopped in mid-air. April could see Blue Suit and Beige Suit, swinging gently, almost halfway up. Blue Suit was pointing to the tow tower above him with his ski pole. What a time for a tow to break! With tears in her eyes, April headed for the lodge.

"Aunt Nora, the tow's broken down again," she said, as she slid behind the snack bar. "I'll take over in here if you want to help."

"I'd better," was all her aunt said, slipping her arms into her ski jacket, and jamming her toque on her head as she ran out the door.

A few minutes later, while she was serving four cups of hot chocolate to a woman and her kids, April heard the welcome whir of the tow coming to life. Whew, she breathed, that's better. Aunt Nora returned in another moment, and slid behind the snack bar with a sigh.

"Just a slipped gear," she said, shaking her head. "We were supposed to change all those gears this winter!"

April wondered if her aunt had seen Blue Suit and Beige Suit on the hill. She had a feeling her aunt would be very surprised to see them, even if Uncle Neil wasn't.

CHAPTER ELEVEN

A Little Help From Your Friends

===========================

She didn't have to wait too long to find out. A short time later the lodge door banged open and Karen came bursting through, her face glowing with excitement. Behind her, looking calm and amused, were Blue Suit and Beige Suit.

"Mom!" called Karen.

"Mrs. Hearst," said Beige Suit, stepping forward with his smooth English charm. "How pleasant to see you again."

April glanced at her aunt. A slow flush was spreading up her neck. Aunt Nora was clearly not taken in by smooth English manners.

"May I ask what you are doing here?" she asked coldly.

"Mom!" cried Karen. "Listen! They want to sponsor me... pay everything... my travel expenses, new racing skis, the on-snow camp in Alberta with the Canadian team! Mr. Delorac knows the national coach," Karen could hardly get the words out, she was so excited.

"Oh really?" was Aunt Nora's reply. "And why would they do that?"

"Mom!" pleaded Karen. Everything that she

wanted so badly was suddenly within her grasp. Money, new equipment, a chance for professional coaching—everything that stood between her and winning was about to be swept aside! April couldn't help knowing what it meant to her.

"We came to watch your daughter ski," Beige Suit said. "We've heard she's *practically* certain to make the Divisional Team this year." His stress on 'practically' was faint, but you couldn't miss it, April thought. These guys were smooth!

"And they say it might be possible to get tutoring, too, Mom," Karen bubbled. "That way I could miss school and still get my year, and go to all the races, even OUT WEST!"

"Just a minute, Karen," Aunt Nora held up her hand. "What do you think of my daughter's abilities?" she asked, looking from Blue Suit to Beige Suit.

"Well, she's excellent, of course," Blue Suit drawled. "With the right sort of opportunities — some European experience—definitely championship material."

"Switzerland!" breathed Karen, her face rapt.

"Ahem," broke in Beige Suit, clearing his voice. He had a wide, tanned, movie star's face, April thought, and a deep voice like an announcer. "Mrs. Hearst. We're trying to establish our firm in skiing in this area . . ."

"You're trying to get our property, because you need it for your development," said Aunt Nora quickly.

"*Purchase* your property, Madam, and for a very fair price," said Blue Suit at once.

"And part of this very fair *purchase* price, I

suppose, would be all these wonderful things you are going to do for Karen?" The flush had climbed to Aunt Nora's cheeks now, but her eyes remained steady and clear.

"Money... equipment... the right people, my dear Mrs. Hearst," said Blue Suit. "Is it possible to reach the top in skiing without them?"

"Maybe not," said Aunt Nora. She turned to look at Karen, who was suddenly growing pale. "It's certainly easier to get there if you have them..." Her voice was very steady, but April could see the pain in her face as she looked at Karen's.

They've both worked so hard, April thought. These guys really know how to go for a person's weak spot! April had been amazed, ever since she'd arrived at Snowbird Mountain, at how much they had all been willing to sacrifice so that Karen could become a champion. She held her breath, wondering if Aunt Nora would be willing to sacrifice even Snowbird itself for their dream.

"The only trouble is," Aunt Nora said slowly, still looking at Karen, "if you didn't make it... with all the money and the fancy equipment, bought... at this price... " She gestured around the lodge, at the smooth round logs, the long tables loaded with ski equipment, the sun streaming in the windows. "Then what would you have left?"

"I know I'll make it," Karen whispered.

"Of course you will!" Aunt Nora shook her head briskly. "Since you've involved the whole family in this matter," she said to Blue Suit, "it will have to be a family decision."

"We're not in any great rush," said Blue Suit smiling. April could see him mentally rubbing his hands with glee. He was sure now the Hearsts would sell. "It's your daughter who is running out of time, isn't it?" He smiled again, very unpleasantly, at Karen.

I'd like to kick his teeth in, thought April. These guys always make me feel so violent! They're so sure of themselves! She watched them stride to the door, pulling on their ski mitts. Beige Suit gave the door frame a pat as he went out, as though he already owned it.

"We'll talk about this after dinner," was all Aunt Nora said, as she turned back to the grill, where two meat patties were turning into cinders. "Karen, you have a training schedule to keep to."

"I'm going," Karen said, her voice nearly breaking.

Dinner, served at nearly eight, after all the cleaning up and putting away was finished, was a quiet meal. Danny stayed, as usual on Saturday nights, so he would be there when the tow opened on Sunday. April could tell he knew. Nobody felt like eating much, though they had all spent a hard day in the open air.

After dinner Uncle Neil lit a fire in the wood stove, and pulled all the chairs up close. As the birch logs burst into flame with a hiss and crackle of burning silver bark, he looked from one anxious face to another.

"I might as well start this by telling you all that I *had* decided to sell," he said.

"What!" burst out three surprised voices at once.

"April guessed, I think," said Uncle Neil. "Those men were cutting trees on crown land that day you saw them—the cross-country trail is mostly on government land—but still I should have chased them off. . ."

"Neil! What are you talking about?" interrupted Aunt Nora, looking up at her tall husband in amazement.

"About three weeks ago, I went to see the bank about an extension on the mortgage," he said. "They won't give us one. I'm sure Roy Wilkins, the manager, would have, but he's being pressured too. I decided that it was better to sell Snowbird Mountain than just lose it. I didn't know how to tell you," he said, looking again from one to the other. "I was stalling. Nora, you and I own this property jointly, so actually the deal couldn't go through unless you agreed too."

He stirred the blazing fire with the poker, sending up an angry shower of sparks. "I didn't know how I'd convince you it was the right thing to sell," he went on. "Snowbird has always been your home . . . your dad built it." Aunt Nora stared into the fire.

"But they knew how to get to you and Karen," Uncle Neil said, giving the fire another savage poke. "That *bribe* they offered Karen today was the meanest, lowest, most miserable piece of business I've ever seen . . ." Uncle Neil's voice was rising, getting louder.

"I've just been wondering all afternoon how I was so weak-minded as to give in to them!" April sat up. She stared at her uncle. The fire was reflected in his eyes, but they were blazing too. "I guess I've just been working too hard, and letting myself get tired," he said. "But I'll tell you one thing. They won't get Snowbird Mountain without a fight! I won't sign that agreement to sell, even if you do, Nora!"

Aunt Nora stood up and threw herself into his arms. There was a long pause, and April shared a look of relief with Danny. Then her uncle and aunt turned to Karen.

"What about it, daughter?" Uncle Neil said.

"What if they're right, Dad?" Karen asked. "What if there is no way to the top without money and influence?"

"I don't think they're right," said Uncle Neil slowly. "But, unfortunately, what I think doesn't really matter. The only ones who can prove they're wrong are you and Danny. I'll fight to keep this roof over our heads and that hill under your skis; and you fight to prove you can win races with talent and hard work!"

Now it was Karen's turn to gaze into the fire. All her dreams of skiing in Switzerland, working out with the national team, flying down race courses on skis custom-designed for her, were going up in smoke.

And April, for her part, wished with all her heart that there was something—anything—she could do to help. She and her dad had never worried about money in Vancouver. There was always enough for food and rent and that was all they really needed. There were no mortgages to pay, no machines to keep running. Dad had always talked about 'having a little nest egg in the bank', but they'd never managed to save enough money to build the nest, let alone hatch an egg! I wish I had a nest egg now, she thought, her chin on her hand as she watched the steadily burning fire, to give Uncle Neil.

She looked up at the faces around the fireplace. Uncle Neil, with his arm still around Aunt Nora, looked relieved that his secret was out in the open. Aunt Nora's small face looked determined and proud and worried, all at the same time. Danny and Karen, in the twin armchairs, were obviously sharing the same thoughts of victory at the second Challenge Cup race in Sudbury in two weeks.

Suddenly, there was a knock on the back door, the door that led to the parking lot and was seldom used. Uncle Neil looked curiously at Aunt Nora, and then went to answer it. A gust of snow let in Blue Suit himself, Mr. Delorac.

"Yes . . . ?" said Uncle Neil, without stepping back from the door. "Can I help you?"

"I . . . uh . . . could I step in for a moment?" Blue Suit had edged his way in, but Uncle Neil left the door open, and snow continued to blow around him and into the room.

"Uh . . . it's snowing quite hard," said Mr. Delorac. The snow blowing in around him seemed to make it difficult for him to keep up his smooth line of chat.

"That's all right," said Uncle Neil. "What was it you wanted?"

"Well, I had some further details I thought your wife and uh . . . daughter . . . might be interested in . . ."

Karen stood up and pulled down her ski

sweater with a sharp tug. "Not interested!" she said clearly, tossing back her blond hair with a shake of her head.

"Oh...I...uh...see," said Blue Suit. A hard gust of wind suddenly swept in a large amount of snow. It was beginning to drift around his aprés-ski boots.

"I hope you do," said Uncle Neil coldly. "Snowbird Mountain, *for the last time*, is not for sale! My family is not interested in your offer... none of your offers!"

"I'm sure you'll change your mind..." Blue Suit started to say.

"Not even if you stand there talking till you freeze to death!" Uncle Neil said.

April thought that would be a fitting end to Mr. Blue Suit. Although the room was growing cold, April was glowing inside. Uncle Neil had called them his 'family', and here, around the warmth of the fire, she knew they *were* a family!

Mr. Delorac turned his snow-covered back angrily on Uncle Neil and disappeared into the storm.

"Way to go!" said Danny, as Uncle Neil shut and bolted the door.

"Let's hope that's the end of him!" Aunt Nora said fervently.

"Oh I don't think it will be the end of him," Uncle Neil shook his head slowly. "He'll be back, with his friend—and others, no doubt. They've made up their minds they want Snowbird Mountain, and people like that don't give up easily!"

CHAPTER TWELVE

Ski School

Sundays were Ski School days at Snowbird, and as they waited for the big yellow buses to roll in, full of noisy eager kids, Danny, April and Karen sat in a row on a picnic bench in the lodge, putting on their ski boots.

"I hate teaching those little jam-lickers!" Karen said, pounding her heel into her boot and snapping up the buckles. "They can never find their skis, they can never do up their boots, and they're always getting cold."

"Those little jam-lickers, as you call them, are the racing champions a few years from now," Aunt Nora reminded her, coming over with the class lists in her hand. "You and Danny take the two Nancy Greene classes. Their try-outs are next week, and they're just as excited about that as you are about the Challenge Cup."

"Yeah, remember," Danny said, "when the Snowbird team won the Nancy Greene championship for all of Northern Ontario? We thought it was really big time!" He stood up and leaned forward in his boots to see if they were tight enough.

"Speaking of the try-outs, April," Aunt Nora suddenly said, "I'd like to get you on the team."

"Me!" April sat up straight on the picnic bench.

"Yes, you. You'll race against the other kids from the ski school next weekend, and we'll pick a team to compete with the Nancy Greene skiers from other clubs. It's a good way to get started racing, and I think you're ready."

"Good for you, Ape," Danny cheered.

Karen turned angrily to Danny. "I think it's ridiculous!" she cried. "All the kids will be a lot younger than she is. She's going to feel *stupid*!"

"No," Aunt Nora said calmly. "There'll be others her age on the team."

"But Mom." Karen protested, "she has no experience!"

What's going on here, April wondered, staring at her furious cousin. Doesn't she *want* me to race?

"Lots of kids don't start until they're April's age," Danny said. "How old are you, kid? Twenty-five, did you say?"

"Well, I think it's dumb," Karen insisted, glaring at Danny. "She's only been able to make it down the hill without falling for a week!"

"Karen, that's enough," Uncle Neil said quietly, coming up behind them.

Just then the front door burst open and the horde of tramping, giggling, shouting kids exploded into the lodge. Karen groaned and stalked off muttering, "Stupid! She's going to make a fool of herself with these kids!"

"You mustn't mind Karen," Uncle Neil said.

But April did mind. "I don't know, Aunt Nora," she said, looking around at all the kids so confidently getting into their ski gear. "Maybe I am too old to start . . ."

But Aunt Nora was still staring after Karen. "I don't know what's wrong with her . . ." she said, sounding worried.

"If you ask me," Danny shrugged, "she's getting jealous because our little friend here is skiing so well."

Karen, jealous of my skiing, April thought, now *that's* a joke!

"Whatever it is," Aunt Nora said, "I don't want anyone making excuses for her. April, I want you to get out there and train today. We'll *all* take turns in the snack bar." There was fire in her eyes as she went off to tell Karen.

"And just remember Crazy Jim Jefferson," Danny grinned.

"Who?"

"Crazy Jim Canuck, they called him. Put on his first pair of skis when he was fifteen, and three years later was on the Canadian Olympic Team."

"No way . . ."

"Sure, there's lots of stories like that. Don't think Karen knows everything there is to know about skiing. Just get out there and give it a whirl. The Nancy Greene Races are a lot of fun, you'll see. The whole team skis for their mountain, not as individuals. Two years ago when Snowbird won—that was the biggest thrill of my short life!"

Just then a six-year-old stuck his foot under April's nose. "Hey . . . can you do up my boot?" he asked.

April grinned at Danny. "Looks like we'd better get to work."

"Okay, but don't forget what I said, eh?" Danny made the thumbs up signal. "Go for it!"

Maybe I will, April thought, as she struggled with the little boy's boot. Maybe I will.

But Karen, when she came in to relieve April in the snack bar, was full of sarcasm. "I hear you let Mother and Danny talk you into the Nancy Greenes. They're all waiting for you out there, your little teammates," she said. She had barely spoken to April since their breakfast quarrel a few weeks ago. And it's better when we *don't* talk to each other, April thought, feeling her anger rising. She thinks I'll make a fool of myself and the whole family, but I'll show her!

April trained like a demon that day, skiing the slalom course Uncle Neil had set over and over. And the next morning she woke determined to get herself into top shape before the try-outs on Saturday. I have to make up for lost time, she thought. What can I do? She ran across the cold pine floor in the loft and stood on her toes to look out the window. The sun was almost up—it was late in January and the days were getting longer. I might even have time to get around the cross-country trail before our bus leaves, April thought, getting swiftly dressed in warm cotton underwear, turtleneck sweater, and ski pants. She noticed happily that her clothes were getting looser with all the exercise.

Downstairs, Uncle Neil was just starting to bang around with the kitchen stove. The living room fireplace burned all night with its airtight

doors shut, and it was still cozy and warm in there as April pulled on her wool ski socks and cross-country boots.

Uncle Neil looked up in surprise as she came into the kitchen. "It's only a quarter to seven," he said. "I thought we'd have to blast you out of bed this morning."

"Can I go cross-country?" April asked.

"Before breakfast?" Uncle Neil sounded astonished. He knew how April loved her breakfast.

"I'm training for the Nancy Greenes."

Uncle Neil bent over the stove to light it. "Well," he said slowly, "I guess so. But take my watch. Don't stay out past seven-thirty. That means twenty minutes out, and twenty back."

April hurried into her wind shell, put a light coat of green wax on her skis, corked and smoothed it, and set off down the trail.

The woods were so quiet and beautiful on a winter morning just before sunrise, that April felt as if she were in a magic place. Her skis whispered along in the grooves of the trail, and here and there rabbit tracks criss-crossed her path.

April concentrated on planting her poles, getting her stride, and keeping her balance. In no time she was warm. By the time she got back to the lodge, the sun had risen behind her—a big orange ball sitting between two snowy hills.

"Ready for breakfast now, eh?" Uncle Neil grinned, as she came in.

The kitchen was cozy. The kettles on the woodstove steamed, and bacon was frying on the big cast iron griddle.

"Mmm, bacon!" April sighed. "It smells so good." One of the best things about winter, she thought, was coming in from that cold icy world to the warm lodge, full of the smell of frying bacon and hot buttered toast!

"You did the whole circuit?" Uncle Neil asked.

"Yup," April answered, her mouth full of toast.

"Good. That was about thirty-five minutes exactly. Take my watch again tomorrow and see if you can trim a couple of minutes off that."

April nodded, as she helped herself to bacon and hot chocolate from the stove. "Will it help my downhill skiing?" she asked.

"Sure thing," Uncle Neil grinned. "Great for building up your legs. Want some more bacon?"

"Sure!" April held up her plate.

At that moment Karen appeared, dressed for school. "I haven't got time for breakfast," she said pointedly, looking at April's plate.

"You have a few extra minutes," Uncle Neil said. "I can give you a lift this morning. I have to go to the bank."

That's right, April thought, munching her bacon. Uncle Neil's all dressed up again in his shirt and tie. But this time, there was no fear about him going to the bank. He'd said he'd never sell Snowbird, and she was sure he would keep his word.

"We've done such great business since that Christmas blizzard," Uncle Neil said, "I think the bank's going to be happy to carry us for a while. Who knows? A couple more good weekends like the last two and we might even get our new tow this winter."

But as soon as they opened the big wood door to the lodge that night after school, April and Karen knew something had gone wrong. The kitchen stoves were out, and the big room was dark and cold. The sound of anxious voices came from behind the living room door. April and Karen looked quickly at one another. This sudden spurt of fear was something, at least, they shared. Together they quietly crossed the pine floor and stood for a moment at the door, listening.

"They can't do that!" Aunt Nora's voice was fierce and low.

"They *have* done it," the girls heard Uncle Neil say. "The mortgage is foreclosed and if we can't come up with the whole amount in sixty days, we lose Snowbird Mountain."

"But that's over ten thousand dollars!" Aunt Nora cried. "Where can we get that kind of money?" The two girls glanced at one another again. Karen gently pushed open the door and walked in, with April behind her.

Aunt Nora looked up but didn't seem to see them. She and Uncle Neil were at the big round dining table, papers and documents spread out around them. "We've been behind on payments before," Aunt Nora said. "They've always been able to arrange something. . . an extension. . ." She waved her hands.

"No more arrangements," Uncle Neil said softly. "No more extensions. I'm afraid our developers have had a little talk with the bank manager. And with the other banks in town too. It seems nobody wants to lend me money." He turned to see the two thunderstruck faces behind him. "I'm sorry you had to hear this," he said to Karen and April. "But you'll have to know the truth sooner or later."

"But there must be some way," Aunt Nora said desperately. "We've got to keep trying!"

"Of course we'll keep trying to raise the money," Uncle Neil told her, but April could tell he thought it would be very difficult.

"If I win . . ." Karen suddenly said, in a low fierce voice like her mother's. "If I win *every* race, and I'm Canadian Juvenile Champion this year, and I'm from Snowbird Mountain, they won't dare close us down! Somebody out there" — she waved her arms as if to indicate the whole of the world outside their little corner of Northern Ontario — "somebody will back us up!" Her face had that white, determined look again.

"You mustn't count on that," Uncle Neil said, reaching for his daughter's hand. "Business, and banks — that's something different from winning ski races."

"I don't believe you!" Karen said coldly, staring at him. The whole room seemed full of her desire to win, and Uncle Neil's worry. April remembered how her dad had always laughed at money problems. He'd just moved, if he couldn't pay the rent, shopped at the Salvation Army when he was between jobs. How different this all was! Snowbird Mountain was both a job *and* a home for the Hearsts, and something more, too. Dad would say it's not good to care about one thing, or one place, so much, April thought, if it gets you into a fix like this. But — she looked around at the stone fireplace with its trophies, the low windows heaped with snow, the braided rugs on the floor — I care too!

"I don't want everyone crawling around here looking lower than a bug's eyebrow," Uncle Neil said. "I'm going to see the Member of Parliament for this area and try to get some government help for Snowbird." He looked around at the sober faces. "And in the meantime why don't we concentrate on what Snowbird Mountain's all about — skiing. Karen, you and Danny have the Challenge Cup next weekend, and April has the Nancy Greene try-outs on Saturday."

CHAPTER THIRTEEN

Wings on Her Heels

April had green butterflies on trampolines in her stomach when she woke Saturday morning and realized that *this* was the day. Aunt Nora, luckily, seemed to understand that April had no appetite for breakfast. "Take these scraps out to the birds," Aunt Nora said, handing her a cake pan full of bread crusts and birdseed, "and see what kind of a day it is."

April put on boots and parka and stepped into the light powder snow. It was going to be a marvellous day. The sun was just lighting the snow, and golden ice crystals danced in the air. The chickadees, always first up, were already hopping around the bird feeder Uncle Neil had nailed to the big pine tree at one end of the lodge. April brushed the new snow off the shelves and a little black-capped chickadee flew up and perched lightly on her shoulder for just a second. April laughed and dumped the cake pan on the clean shelf as he flew away scolding "chickadee-dee-dee!"

"Was that for good luck?" she laughed. "Because I'll need it!"

But the fresh air had given her a better appetite, and she managed to polish off a few pieces of French toast with wild blueberry syrup before helping her aunt with the dishes and getting into an old, outgrown racing suit of Karen's.

She didn't particularly relish wearing Karen's hand-me-downs, but the smooth pants and jacket did feel a lot less bulky than her normal ski suit. She looked at her image in the long mirror in Aunt Nora's bedroom. Her long, red-brown hair was pulled back in a ponytail, and her short body looked much slimmer in the racing suit. Hey, she told her serious, rosy-tanned face, you look almost like a ski-racer! She'd had plenty of opportunity to study the faces on Karen's ski posters before the blanket wall went up, and they all seemed to have that tanned, bright-eyed intensity.

As she came back into the kitchen, she could hear Karen's voice, raised angrily, arguing with her mother.

"A whole perfect day of skiing wasted on this baby stuff!" she shouted. "The best chance I have to train before the Challenge next week, and you want me to blow it, helping with these *stupid* Nancy Greenes. It's not fair!"

"You didn't think the Nancy Greenes were stupid a couple of years ago, when you were racing in them," Aunt Nora reminded her. She kept her voice calm, but April could hear the anger in it.

She by-passed the kitchen battleground, and

went on into the big front room of the lodge. The sun was streaming through the windows, glowing on the warm cedar walls and picnic tables. April wished passionately that Karen would not wreck this beautiful day for her. Let the old snob go and practise by herself on the far side of Snowbird Mountain, April thought. Who needs her?

But the stormy battle continued from the kitchen. April could hear it clearly through the open lunch counter. "Danny's coming over..." Karen cried. "It's not fair... you don't care if we win!"

"Danny usually remembers that things at Snowbird are a group effort," Aunt Nora said. "It's not just one person or two who are important."

"The Challenge Cup! That's what's important!" came Karen's agonizing cry.

April couldn't stand any more. She grabbed her boots quickly and headed outdoors. She was just in time to meet the Snowbird Mountain Ski School bus as it came rolling and crunching into the parking lot. The colourfully dressed kids came tumbling off, as they usually did, and the whole noisy, laughing, scrambled-up bunch surged towards the lodge door. That, April thought with a sigh, will sure put a stop to the argument inside. Karen will have something else to do besides complain!

Uncle Neil appeared on the ski dozer and hopped down to greet the skiers. The unhappy atmosphere of only a few moments ago vanished in the bright winter air and the bubbly excitement of the young Nancy Greene contestants. Everyone from eight to thirteen tried out for the Snowbird Mountain team, April knew. This was where everybody started. It *was* exciting!

The trouble was, most of the racers her age had been skiing since they were four or five, and racing at least three years. April confided her fears to Danny when he came into the shack with numbers for all of them to wear over their jackets.

"So they know what they're doing, and you're faking it . . ." Danny grinned his wicked grin at her.

"But I've never skied until this winter!"

"They don't know that! You'll be the mystery girl . . . out of nowhere you just come swooping in and beat them all!" Danny ruffled her smooth dark hair. "Just put a little more elbow grease into that wax job you're doing . . . and you might make it all the way down the hill."

He's impossible! April thought, but he makes you feel better every time. She went at her polishing job with a ferocious energy, smoothing the bottoms of her skis until they felt like satin. Then she worked her feet into the snug ski boots, did up the buckles carefully from bottom to top, bent her knees and leaned forward to make sure they felt right on the fronts of her ankles . . . and was ready for the first run.

They had drawn lots to see in which order they would ski. It was better to come first, or nearly first, before the snow was rutted by the other racers. April drew eighth . . . about the middle.

From the tow, April could see the course, two pairs of poles with red flags, zig-zagging down the face of the hill.

At the top of the tow, April slid off and joined the cluster of other racers near the starting gate. Most of them had seen her around the lodge, (behind the snack bar usually, April thought ruefully), and they looked at her with undisguised curiosity as she skied up to them.

"I didn't know you raced, April," said a deep-voiced girl named Donna, who was in April's grade six class. April remembered Danny's advice. She decided to be mysterious.

"Sometimes..." she mumbled.

"She's from B.C., knucklehead," said a boy in a blue racing suit. "You know... B.C.? Where Nancy Greene *comes from*?"

Everybody nodded and looked impressed. Donna tossed her head and shut up. Thanks, April thought, smiling at the boy in blue. I couldn't have said it better myself.

The skiers worked their way slowly down the hill, studying the course, deciding the best way to enter and the fastest path to the bottom. It was here, Uncle Neil said, that concentration was so important. You had to memorize the positions of those poles, and how you would run them... have that picture burned into your mind.

As she crouched in the starting gate half an hour later, April tried to remember everything she'd been taught about getting off to a fast start. She dug her poles deep in the snow, and set her legs to spring forward as she strained to hear the starting signal.

"Go!" The shout rang in the clear cold air. April shot forward. Move! she urged herself, skate hard for the first set of poles, make a high turn through the gate, now here's the pitch, pick up speed, here's the hairpin, CAREFUL, do two turns tight together, GET CONTROL! One more gate . . . keep low, keep the weight on your downhill ski! GO, GO! FASTER! April wasn't sure when she crossed the finish line, but suddenly realized there were no more red-flagged poles ahead, just a blur of spectators.

She did a wide turn and stopped, gasping for breath. April saw Danny come swooping towards her from the timekeeper's stand, waving a ski pole wildly in the air. "Fantastic," he cried, "twenty-one point five seconds . . . April, that was just fantastic." He clumped her on the back and danced on his skis.

"Was that . . . a good time?" stammered April. Her mind was still spinning down the hill, soaring through the gates, as though she had wings on her heels.

"Good?" he shouted. "Good? Just five seconds better than anyone else so far, that's how good. I'm telling you, Ape, I saw Crazy Jim Jefferson when you came flying down that hill!"

"I think I can do it faster," said April eyeing the hill. "Do I get another chance?"

Danny pulled her ski hat down over her eyes. "You sure do, champ!"

Each skier had three chances to trim precious seconds from their time and April would never forget the exhilaration of speeding through the course, pushing herself to do it faster and better.

Afterward the kids gathered around to congratulate her. 'The kid who came out of nowhere' as Danny had said, and skied one of the best times all day! Uncle Neil grinned proudly as he posted the names of skiers chosen for the Nancy Greene team, with April's near the top.

Then there was cocoa and hotdogs in the warm lodge, the tow bars swung to a stop, and tired racers pulled off heavy boots, packed up their belongings, and trooped off to the buses.

It was only then that April realized she hadn't seen Karen all day. And I don't care what she feels about me making the team, she thought in astonishment. The thrill of racing had blocked everything else from April's mind, even Karen.

"She's got a stomachache," Aunt Nora explained. "I sent her to bed." April couldn't resist an inward grin. So that's how the battle ended, she thought. Karen gets a day in bed, instead of helping with the races, *or* training.

"I hope the rest does her good." Uncle Neil looked worried.

"I think it will," Aunt Nora answered grimly, and that was all she said.

April hated the thought of going to bed upstairs in the loft—of facing the icy frost of Karen's anger.

Unexpectedly, Uncle Neil came to the rescue. "Well, we don't want April catching whatever it is Karen's got," he said. "Maybe you should sleep down here on the couch tonight . . ." He looked doubtful, as though anyone would hate to sleep on the couch.

April thought of the warm firelit room, the big old velvet couch with its rumpled soft blue cushions—as close to heaven as you could get.

"Oh, I don't think April would catch what

Karen has . . . ," Aunt Nora said in the same grim tone. "But if you'd like to sleep down here," she went on, "of course it's all right."

April flushed. She hated Aunt Nora to suspect how she felt about Karen. "It might be . . . nice and warm . . . ," she said lamely.

"I'll get the spare bedding," Aunt Nora said, uncurling from her big chair and going to the linen closet under the stairs.

Nothing more was said, but all the next week April slept on the old blue couch in the living room. It meant that it was easier to get up in the morning with her uncle, do some warm-up exercises on the rug in front of the fireplace, put her outdoor gear over her PJ's and go out for her early morning cross-country ski. Each day the time got shorter, and she had longer to linger over a nice hot cup of cocoa before it was time to dash up to the loft to dress in school clothes and catch the bus.

Karen was busy every spare moment, training for the second Challenge Cup race in Sudbury. April hardly saw her, except for the rides home in the truck. Then Uncle Neil and Karen talked, and April looked out the window.

Karen said nothing about having her loft to herself, and April noticed that she barely spoke to her mother either. April couldn't help feeling guilty about that, as if their argument had somehow been her fault.

Wednesday night at supper, however, Aunt Nora suddenly said, "Karen, they've found billets for you in Sudbury, so we won't have to stay at a motel."

"Oh NO!" Two bright spots of colour appeared on Karen's cheeks. "I hate staying with some *snobby* family. It'll throw me off in my races, I know it will!"

"Karen!" said Uncle Neil angrily. "You've always had terrific billets — people who have taken a lot of trouble to make you comfortable. Please, don't talk like that!"

"It's very generous of the Fredericksons to offer, and we can't afford motels, so the matter is settled!" said Aunt Nora, her brown eyes flashing back at Karen's wide blue ones.

"I can't stand it!" Karen stood up suddenly and flung herself away from the table. "I can't stand being always *poor*!" she cried, running up the loft stairs.

It's getting to be a regular thing — Karen's running away, April thought, wondering how her cousin could be so wrapped up in herself that she didn't see the pain she was causing her parents. Uncle Neil hadn't said anything about getting the loan to pay off Snowbird Mountain's debt at the bank, and the days were trickling slowly by.

April wondered if they'd be evicted in March, like a family she'd seen a picture of in the Vancouver newspaper — put out on the highway with all their belongings and no place to go. The thin lines around Uncle Neil's mouth, and the shadows under Aunt Nora's eyes seemed to deepen every day.

=========
CHAPTER FOURTEEN
=========

The Second Challenge

=========================

On Thursday night, as Uncle Neil, Danny, Karen, and April drove three hundred kilometres south and west towards Sudbury the rain started to fall.

"We're getting our big January thaw," the owner of the gas station near Sudbury told them. "Snow's almost gone."

The three skiers looked at each other in horror. No snow!

"Supposed to freeze up hard tonight, like," the man went on. "But it's mild enough now, eh?"

"Too mild!" Karen blurted out, dismayed.

"Can't be too mild for me," the old man grinned. "I've seen enough of winter."

"Don't worry, kids," Uncle Neil said as they got back in the truck. "The hill at Adanac faces north—they'll have snow left. And I'm sure anyway they have artificial snow-making equipment."

"I hate artificial snow," Karen said in a low voice. "Dad . . . I've got a bad feeling about this race . . ."

126

"You're too wound up about it, that's all," Uncle Neil said, turning off the highway and onto a residential street. "Try to relax. We'll have a good dinner and then I'll drop you off at your billet."

But neither April nor Karen could relax. The Frederickson's house was too quiet and clean, the bedroom too big and bare, for either of them to feel comfortable.

Next morning at breakfast, April felt as though she might choke getting her shredded wheat down her throat. There's one thing, she thought, looking at the long, sombre faces of Dr. Frederickson and his wife, no fear about Karen looking like a black storm cloud. She fits right in around here. Karen wore her usual frown of furious pre-race concentration, as she steadily and mechanically ate her breakfast. Uncle Neil's sudden ringing of the doorbell made them all jump in the silent breakfast room.

It was a cold sunny day outside, with a sharp wind from the north.

"Will John Bukowski be here today?" Karen asked as they climbed into the truck.

"No, I believe he had to go to the Fleishman Cup race in Quebec this weekend. Sorry," Uncle Neil said, looking at Karen's disappointed face. The storm cloud got heavier.

The sight of the Adanac ski hill did nothing to raise anyone's spirits. It was really just a lump of bare black rock, slightly higher than the other lumps around it, and set at the end of a street of suburban houses. Worse, as they turned into the parking lot and peered up at it through the wind-

127

shield, they could see the sun glaring on a smooth sheet of ice. The melting snow had frozen hard overnight. The thaw, as the gas station man had predicted, was over.

On the deck of the chalet, young skiers and their coaches were busily filing ski edges as sharp as they could make them, to give the racers some control on the icy snow. A ski-dozer, equipped with a special studded rake to break up the polished crust, chugged across the face of the hill. April shuddered as she looked up at it.

"Glad you're not in this one?" Danny said, coming up beside her.

"It looks . . . dangerous," April started to say, when someone came up behind them and thumped Danny on the shoulder.

It was Todd.

"Going to be a different story tomorrow, eh, Danny-boy?" Todd sneered. "*This* is *my* hill!"

"Oh, so *this* is *your* hill," returned Danny. "I wondered where you learned to ski. I thought maybe it was someone's back yard." He looked over his shoulder at the nearby houses.

"We'll see, birdbrain!" Todd muttered, turning away.

April smothered a laugh in her mittened hand.

"I wish he wouldn't take it so personally," Danny said, looking after Todd's swaggering figure. "But since he does . . . oh well! Want to help me file my edges, Ape?"

He showed her how to set the file at the right angle, and use the right light quick stroke, and how to run the side of your thumb down the edge to make sure it was right. Then he went to help Karen. He was back in a moment, shaking his head.

"Boy, is she in a wonderful mood today," he said. "Must have caught it from Todd. What's been happening at Snowbird Mountain, anyway?"

"Didn't Uncle Neil tell you about the bank?" April asked, surprised.

"He mentioned something about the mortgage but I didn't understand," Danny said, looking at her with eyes that were suddenly serious. "We've been having money problems for a long time . . . three bad years . . ."

"I guess this is worse," April said. "And those developers are mixed up in it somehow. But maybe you should ask Uncle Neil about it."

"Maybe he'd tell me to mind my own business," Danny said. "I wish there was something we could do."

"Karen thinks if you guys win races and go to the National Championships at Fortress Mountain . . ."

"Money will fall from heaven? I think she's dreaming! But that explains why she's so weird, all of a sudden. She wants to win too badly."

Karen passed at that moment, throwing them a dark look.

"Whew!" said Danny. "Misery on the march. What did we do?"

"Not *we*," April said, looking after her. "ME!"

"You been putting cracker crumbs and wet toads in her bed again, Ape?"

"I haven't . . ." April began.

"I know, I know, you're a perfectly innocent little kid! Listen, I've got little brothers and sisters, you know, little monsters," Danny grinned and quit teasing. "But you're not like them. I'm going to have a talk with her about this, up at the top." He pointed to the hill. "That is, if she'll speak to me."

But Karen wouldn't talk, not then, or during the whole long day of training, or at dinner in the Steak House, or back in the cold silent Frederickson bedroom. It was as if she'd built an icy wall around herself. Her face was closed, her eyes withdrawn. After all the stormy outbursts of the last few months, this was a new and frightening Karen.

April lay under the starched sheets and wished she'd stayed back at Snowbird Mountain with Aunt Nora. These races were going all wrong. She wasn't to find out how wrong until the next day!

CHAPTER FIFTEEN

Scrap Out!

First, Danny was disqualified. On his first run he missed a gate and was declared out of the race.

"No way!!" Danny shouted shaking his head at the bottom of the hill. "I was sure I was through them all!"

"If you'd spend less time fooling around with her," Karen pointed an angry ski pole at April, "and concentrate on what you're supposed to be doing, it wouldn't happen!"

April glanced up at her cousin and suddenly knew the storm clouds were about to break. She recognized those burning cheeks. She wished herself anywhere but caught in the middle of the hurricane.

For Danny was angry too. April had never seen his eyes narrow like that. "Leave April out of it!" he warned.

"That's right. Stick up for her! Take her side! That's what everyone has done since she got dumped on us. Poor little April," she mocked. "I'm so sick of that! I'm so sick of you!" She turned on April. "You've ruined everything! Nothing has gone right since you've come . . . I . . . " Her voice was rising to full thunder, and people around were starting to stare.

"Karen!" Danny tried to stop her, grabbing her arm.

"Leave me alone!" she spat at him. "You're on her side too. Mother, Dad, you, everyone. I hate her!"

Danny and April shrank back, stung by the uncontrolled fury in her voice.

"Will the girls get into position at the starting gate for the beginning of the next race," boomed the loudspeaker. Karen had drawn third, an excellent position. She would have to hurry to get up the tow.

With one last terrible look at Danny and April, she picked up her poles and skated away on her skis towards the tow. April could feel her face stiff with shock. She felt Danny beside her and hoped he wouldn't grab her arm or anything, because if he did she knew she'd break down and cry. But Danny's face, when she stole a look at it, was not full of pity and sympathy for her. Instead, he was staring up the hill at the tow line, where Karen was now just a blue dot.

"She's in big trouble," he said, his voice deep with worry. "That was terrible. I didn't know . . . "

"You didn't know she hated me?" April said bitterly. "Well, she does." April was in no mood to feel sorry for Karen.

"Oh sure, hate! Everybody in my family hates each other all the time. One week I hate Lise, the next week Michelle hates Robert. You know, on and on . . . but not like *that*!" Danny turned to look at her and his face was white. "That's not normal hate, one kid for another."

"Yeah. It's been fun!" April thought now she *would* cry. Danny was not making her feel better.

"Oh sure, it's bad for you. But Karen! She's a different person! You don't know what a big change this is for her. How come your aunt and uncle don't see? They see every little detail wrong in how we ski . . . how come they don't see this?"

"Well, I don't know. They've had a lot to think about . . ." April muttered, but Danny wasn't listening to her. He was staring up the hill at the blue dot nearly at the top.

"I've got to get up there before the race," he said. "I've got to talk to her before she comes down!" He raced down the deck steps, snapped on his skis and was striding away with powerful thrusts of his poles.

April felt numb and cold inside, and wished she were far away from this bare ugly hill, out of the icy wind and the harsh sun. But it was as if her mitts were glued to the rail of the deck, and she was forced to stand there and watch everything that happened on that high white sheet of snow before her.

She saw Danny, crawling slowly up the hill with the others on the tow line, like a line of ants. Saw the first skier flash down between the poles, heard the cheers of the crowd as she crossed the finish line. "C'mon, Marnie, go, GO!" Saw the second racer in the starting gate, and the small blue blur that must be Karen in position near the gate, waiting for her turn.

133

Danny's portion of the tow line disappeared out of sight at the top of the hill, just as the second skier shot into space. April knew he must be skiing off the tow. Everything seemed to be moving in slow motion. The racer, going over eighty kilometres an hour, seemed to float gracefully through her turns. April saw Danny at last, skiing up to Karen just as she made her move to enter the starting gate. Too late for any conversation. Danny, April knew, wouldn't disturb Karen's concentration in the starting gate, no matter what he had to say.

The other racer reached the bottom and a cheer went up again. There was a pause. "The third racer — Karen Hearst — from Snowbird Mountain Club." April clutched the rail.

Karen was moving. She hurtled through the first gate and turned for the next. Picking up speed with every turn, ignoring the ice, shaving the poles close — too close! April wanted to shut her eyes, but she couldn't. She saw Karen lose control as she entered the flush; saw her fall — smashing poles as she slid, skidded, scraped down the awful icy face. There was no soft snow to break the fall or disguise the ugliness of it. At the end of a trail of shattered gates, red and blue poles lying helter-skelter, Karen finally lay, unmoving. Her racing skis, held by their brakes, were far above her on the hill.

Still unable to move, April watched the tiny figures on the hill converge towards that still body. The gatekeepers from the side, the officials from the bottom, and Danny, skiing as though he were racing himself, from the top. There was no

sound from the people gathered on the deck, and then someone said, "Where's Neil Hearst?" and someone answered, "He's up there." And that was all that needed to be said.

The ski patrol had gone into action, bringing the fibreglass sled down to Karen, and in a moment April saw one of them flying down the hill towards the chalet.

"Call for the ambulance," he shouted, when he was near enough to be heard.

Someone near April turned to relay the message inside.

April felt her legs start to shake, and a great turmoil inside as though she were going to be sick. She looked frantically around. There was no one here that she knew. No one who knew she was Karen's cousin or Uncle Neil's neice. No one who would understand why this kid suddenly started to cry and throw up. So she didn't. She just stood there, on the deck, not moving, watching as they brought Karen down on the sled and loaded her into the white ambulance with Uncle Neil and Danny and drove her away.

Fantastically, the race went on. April watched the gatekeepers pick up the broken poles and stick them back in the snow again. She heard the next racer announced and watched a small green dot at the top move into the starting gate. She seemed to stand there forever until she felt a hand on her arm.

"You're April Martineau, aren't you?" It was Todd Hartford again.

April nodded.

"Dan asked me to find you. This is my mom."

Behind Todd stood a tall, striking-looking woman in a black ski suit.

"I can drive you back to your billet," she said kindly.

"Would you mind," April swallowed, "driving me to the hospital?"

"Well, I don't know." April could see that Todd's mother didn't really want to get involved.

"Please!" she said urgently. "I'd like to find out what's happened to my cousin." That other time, when her father had gone to the hospital, and she hadn't gone with him, haunted April.

"Well, I guess so," Mrs. Hartford said. "Get your stuff together, dear. We'll have to find your uncle at the hospital, I suppose. I can't just *drop* you there!"

Todd was looking genuinely sorry. "Bye, April," he said, as she hurried in the wake of his disappearing mother. "I hope Karen's okay."

"Please, let her be okay," April found herself praying, as Mrs. Hartford's car wove its way through Sudbury traffic to the General Hospital. Mrs. Hartford parked illegally in the doctors' spaces and hustled April inside the emergency department. She clearly wanted to get back to the races.

Uncle Neil was not there, but Danny was, sitting rigidly in the waiting room, staring at a folded magazine. April dropped down beside him, so glad to see his familiar face she could hardly stand it.

"Hey, Ape," he managed a pinched smile. "Sorry we left you hanging."

"That's okay," April said quickly. "You didn't,

137

anyway. You told Todd." Mrs. Hartford had already disappeared. "How's Karen?" Danny shook his head.

Suddenly Uncle Neil appeared at the end of the hall. He walked slowly over to them and slumped in a chair. "Her spine's all right," was the first thing he said. "No serious back or neck injuries, as far as they can tell, thank God! But they're pretty sure she has a fractured left tibia and torn ligaments, and maybe a broken collarbone. We're waiting for the X rays." He leaned forward, his elbows resting on his knees, and looked at them. "It's the end of racing for Karen this year, maybe permanently. That's all she's going to care about."

They all knew it was true, that was the terrible thing. And Danny and April shared the same thought. They knew why Karen had raced the way she did, as if she were trying to fly away from herself. They knew.

CHAPTER SIXTEEN

Break-In

==

There was lots more space in the truck going home, and a big empty space in all of them at the thought of Karen, lying alone in her hospital bed, left behind. Danny had hung the gold medal he won in Sunday's final grand slalom race over the end of her bed where she could see it. "This one was for you," he muttered, as he hung it there.

"How . . . was the hill today?" Karen murmured. She looked small and very white amid all the wires and plaster and equipment the hospital had draped around her.

"Fast," Danny said.

"Who won . . . the girls'?" Karen asked. It was painfully obvious that Karen didn't realize how badly she was hurt. Part of her head was still back in yesterday, before the fall, and she wasn't sure yet why she was here, lying so still, with her leg in a cast and her chest all bandaged.

"Oh . . . Tina," Danny answered reluctantly.

"That's enough talk for now," Uncle Neil

interrupted. "We'd better get going. Nora will be on the first bus back to Sudbury, Karen. Don't you worry about anything, okay?"

"When can I come home?" Karen asked, so wistfully that April felt a lump in her throat. She'd hung back near the window through this visit, not sure Karen would want to see her, and not sure what to say. She just couldn't get rid of the feeling that somehow the whole thing had been her fault.

"The doctor says a couple of weeks," Uncle Neil said quietly, taking her hand. And then they'd left, April looking back once at the cold white room and Karen's bewildered blue eyes.

Aunt Nora was flustered and anxious when they arrived at Snowbird Mountain. She started packing at once.

"You just would never believe how busy we were this weekend," she told them as she hurriedly threw a few clothes into a tote bag. "It's so maddening, Neil, to have good skiing now, when it's too late to do any good!"

Uncle Neil was flipping through the book where tow passes for the weekend were recorded in Aunt Nora's neat up-and-down handwriting. "Five hundred sixty tow passes in one weekend!" he said, astonished. "Why couldn't we have had this kind of snow last year, before we got so far behind with our payments!"

"Exactly! And now Karen . . . Just what happened?" She turned to Danny and April, her eyes large and lined with worry in her thin face. "You two were with her just before the race . . . Neil said she skied like a maniac down that hill! Was she upset or anything?"

April looked quickly at Danny, and Danny shrugged—a beautiful, innocent shrug that said nothing. Aunt Nora looked sharply at them but asked no more. As he was leaving, Danny whispered to April, "I figure it's better not to tell them —about the fight. There's nothing they can do about it, and it'll make them feel badly."

April nodded. There *was* nothing Uncle Neil and Aunt Nora could do, except send her away so their family could get back the way it was before she'd been dumped on them. And that would be hard for them to do—there was nowhere for her to go!

With Aunt Nora in Sudbury and Danny home in Iroquois Falls, April and Uncle Neil were left to rattle around Snowbird Mountain by themselves. April moved back upstairs to the loft and took down the blanket. Every time she looked at Karen's empty bunk, she seemed to see her cousin lying there, head thrown back so her long blond hair almost swept the floor. Knees up, arms crossed on her chest—staring at her ski posters on the wall—willing herself to make it—to the Canadian Championships at Whistler, a World Cup race in Austria, the Olympics . . . and April would feel a weight of sadness and guilt that nothing seemed to lift.

"You've quit training," Uncle Neil remarked one morning when the two of them were eating breakfast.

April pushed her pancake around in its pool of syrup. "Yeah. . . I guess it doesn't seem to matter much any more."

"It matters," Uncle Neil said quietly. "I have

to go to Timmins today, and I won't be back until after dinner. But tomorrow," he went on, "after school, we're going to start training again for that next Nancy Greene race."

There was a long silence in the big kitchen.

"Okay?" Uncle Neil asked.

"Okay," April mumbled, wishing he hadn't brought it up.

But, she admitted, as she walked home from the school bus that night, it does seem funny not to rush home to get in some skiing. I miss the view from the top. Soft flakes of fresh snow were falling, and instead of crunching, April's footsteps were whisper quiet. It'll be beautiful skiing tomorrow, she thought, and there was a little hitch in the heavy weight of sadness she was carrying inside.

Suddenly April stopped short. Ahead of her the red gates of Snowbird Mountain were open. They should have been closed, with Uncle Neil away. But they were open, swung carelessly back into the snowbanks at crazy angles.

April started to run. Maybe Uncle Neil was home! She jogged silently through the falling snow, around the corner to the parking lot. There was no gold pick-up. Just a small grey car that looked as though it could go very fast. April stopped, blinking the snowflakes off her eyes, and listened.

There was no sound. April wished she were not alone. Something about that silver car made her shiver. It looked mean, almost bullet-shaped. And it was so quiet here in the woods.

April climbed the snowbank at the end of the

parking lot, and slid down behind the lodge. There were no windows on this north side, and she thought she would like to see whoever was visiting Snowbird, before they saw her.

That turned out to be not so easy. The snow was deeper than April's waist, and she had to crawl, holding onto the wall logs, to reach the kitchen door. Suddenly, something made her stop and try to swallow her heavy breathing, so she could hear.

Someone was on the other side of the log wall. She could hear muffled voices; then, one clearer as it came near the wall.

"... finished here... let's go..." April felt anger and fear rising up in her. Who was in there?

She ploughed furiously through the snow, slid down the bank into the walkway shovelled from the kitchen door, and dove into the little shed where garbage cans and shovels were kept.

She heard the kitchen door creak open.

"... nothing but a big old firetrap, anyway..." She heard a man's voice laugh.

"Yeah... logs must be full of dry rot." The voices stopped suddenly. "Hey, what's this?"

April realized with horror that her scarf had got caught on a nail as she rushed into the shed. Its bright red tassels were hanging outside!

The shed door swung open, and there, to April's astonishment, stood Blue Suit. Behind him was another man in a parka and jeans. He reached around Blue Suit and yanked April out of the shed, tearing her scarf away from the nail. His hand on her ski jacket was as rough and dirty as Blue Suit's was polished and clean.

"Now take it easy, Bill," said Blue Suit in his icy drawl. "This is Miss Martineau, Hearst's niece. We mustn't alarm her!"

"What were you doin' in there?" growled the man in the parka, letting her go.

"Getting a shovel," said April quickly. "It's snowing."

"So it is!" Blue Suit said sarcastically. "And aren't you a useful child, to come home from school and start shovelling right away."

April gulped. "Uncle Neil's not home . . ." she said, as bravely as she could. "How did you get in?"

"Oh, we weren't inside," Blue Suit drawled. "We understand this place will be for sale after all . . . once the bank takes possession in a few weeks. Just looking it over. It's too bad your uncle doesn't sell to me, you know. This way he loses everything!"

April gaped at him. She was sure these cruel words were meant to cover up the truth — that he had broken into the lodge. How she wished Uncle Neil would come!

"The kid's gonna tell him," Bill growled.

"Yes," said Blue Suit smoothly. "By all means tell your uncle we were here, and that we regret he wasn't home for our little inspection of the premises. Why don't you go in now, dear — you look cold. I'm sure you'll find nothing has been disturbed."

He waited, while April fumbled with her key in the lock, and let herself in. Then he and Bill disappeared in the thickly falling snow.

April stood rigid, until she heard the rich purr

of the silver car's engine die away down the road.

"It's true," Uncle Neil said wearily. "There's nothing to prove they were in here." The two of them had just spent an hour searching Snowbird Mountain Lodge from top to bottom for a sign that anything had been disturbed.

"But Uncle Neil!" April cried. "I heard them in the kitchen! I heard the door open and shut!"

"Nothing you can prove," her uncle sighed. "You didn't even see them."

"I know. It's just the word of an eleven-year-old kid against old smoothie Mr. Blue Suit! Oh, how I hate that man! It's not fair that he gets away with all this stuff just because he's rich."

"Rich and powerful," Uncle Neil said grimly. "There's not a bank or loan company, from here to North Bay, that will lend Snowbird Mountain money."

"He can do that?" April said, amazed.

"Nothing we can prove, once more," Uncle Neil said. "But all it takes is a quiet word about how much money his new ski development will bring to this area, and how our old lodge is standing in the way of progress."

"And fancy cars and suits, and a Hollywood haircut," cried April. "Oh Uncle Neil, how I despise that man!"

"Not worth despising," said Uncle Neil, standing up with a stretch. "Let's go drown our sorrows in some hot cocoa, and cheer up! I haven't given up yet. Besides, there's some good news. Nora and Karen are coming home tomorrow."

CHAPTER SEVENTEEN

Friends to the Rescue

Good news? April felt as though a tonne of lead had been dropped around her shoulders. Karen coming home! A Karen in a cast . . . a Karen who couldn't *ski* . . . a Karen who must hate the sight of her! April wondered how on earth she could ever face it.

As it turned out, she didn't have to — because Karen kept her face turned away from all of them. She insisted on being alone in the loft.

"But Karen," Aunt Nora protested, "Neil and I can move to the loft, and you and April can have our room. You'll be closer, and you need a lot of care."

But Karen was not to be persuaded, and Uncle Neil carried her carefully up the loft stairs, and hooked her leg up to the metal contraption they'd brought from the hospital. She had to lie very still at first, so the bones could set.

"Not *that* still, though," Aunt Nora said with a worried frown, as she mixed a batch of muffins in the kitchen. "She just lies there like she did in the hospital, staring at the wall or the TV screen."

April had seen her. She'd tiptoed up for one visit, but found Karen so changed she'd come down again quickly. Karen looked younger, and helpless, and even her shiny hair had lost its vitality.

"It's more than just her leg that's shattered," Uncle Neil said. "It's all her dreams of skiing, Nora."

"They don't need to be," Aunt Nora said, with a worried shake of her head. "Something's hurting her worse than her injuries. I wish I knew what it was!"

April went away to curl up on her soft blue couch and try to sleep. She wrapped Aunt Nora's afghan tightly around her, and hugged one of the big cushions. The sound of Karen's scream 'I hate you . . . you've ruined everything!' sounded in her ears, and when she shut her eyes she could see Karen's body falling . . . smashing through the poles . . . tumbling over and over on the hard, glistening snow. It seemed to April that Karen was screaming and falling at the same time and forever . . .

In the next few days, April managed a half-hearted attempt at training. The light was good enough now to ski almost an hour after she got off the school bus. "I know I'm not ready," April thought. "I just haven't got the concentration to win." She was thinking about this as she stepped off the school bus, and wondering if she should tell Uncle Neil.

Just then an old black car stopped on the other side of the road, the door slammed quickly, and there was Danny, running across the highway to meet her.

"Got a ride from my brother." Danny waved as the black car pulled away. "Thought I'd come over and cheer up the invalid. And how are you, Ape?"

147

"Not so bad."

"Still training? I'll race you to the gate." They set off at an easy jog, April's knapsack full of books banging between her shoulders with every stride. She didn't care. It's amazing, she thought, how things improve when Danny's around. Maybe he *will* be able to cheer Karen up.

They reached the gates, panting and laughing. Danny picked up a handful of snow and lobbed it at April. "Not bad running, for a kid with short legs!" he shouted.

April bent to get a mittful of snow to retaliate. She looked up to see her target weaving back and forth across the snow road. "Can't get me!"

Suddenly April saw a spire of orange flame leap up over the trees. She rubbed the snow out of her eyes. It was still there! "Danny!" she screamed. "Look! Fire!"

"Oh no! You're not going to get me with that old trick . . ."

April had already started running. The pillar of fire was growing . . . throwing black smoke against the white sky. "The lodge!" she screamed. "The lodge is burning!"

Something in April's face as she ran toward him made Danny turn and look, and the sight put rockets under his feet! April tried to keep up, flinging her knapsack aside, but Danny was much faster and had crossed the big parking lot before she reached it.

Uncle Neil's truck was gone. Now she could see that the pillar of fire was shooting out the top of the chimney — high, high into the air.

"It's a chimney fire!" shouted Danny.

148

"Karen's in the loft!" April shouted back. "She's . . . she's all tied up to that metal thing . . . she can't get down!"

Danny threw her a horrified look. Then he disappeared around the corner of the lodge running hard.

As she reached the front door, April saw to her horror that the inside of the lodge was already full of thick, billowing smoke. Inside, the roar of burning chimney was terrible! Somewhere, April heard Danny coughing.

Suddenly he appeared out of the smoke like a ghost, his long scarf dripping wet from the kitchen sink and wound around his mouth and nose.

"Try to get the fire extinguisher," came his muffled voice. "Crawl along the floor to the fireplace. Shut the dampers tight and cut off the air to the fire. Then aim the extinguisher at the ceiling. It must have caught fire or there wouldn't be so much smoke. And don't come up those loft stairs . . . no matter what happens!"

"Danny!" April cried, as he disappeared across the lodge floor in the swirling clouds of smoke.

Then she started to cough too. She tried to fight down panic and remember what he'd said. The fire extinguisher was beside the fireplace, she knew that. Crawl on the floor . . . yes, it was better down there. Crawl across the big front room, through the open door to the living room, past the couch, now reach up along the bricks . . . There! April had the long heavy cylinder in her arms. The roaring of the chimney was loud and fierce.

Close the dampers—shut off air to the fire.

April could see the damper knobs like two evil red eyes through the smoke. Too hot! she thought frantically. Even with mitts . . . too hot! She was coughing furiously now. Better . . . try to put out the fire. She aimed the nozzle at the top of the chimney where it disappeared into the ceiling and pressed the trigger. There was a tremendous WHOOSH as the chemical was released, a hissing as the foam met the red hot pipe and burning wood. She held it as long as she could and then collapsed, coughing.

"April!" she heard a choked cry. "I've got her! Let's get out of here!"

She heard a terrible banging and clatter in the direction of the loft stairs.

"Danny!" she screamed.

"Get out, Ape!" came the strangled answer. "Hurry!"

April put her face as close to the floor as she could and crawled and wriggled her way back through the smoke to the lodge door. She couldn't see Danny or Karen, but she could hear the weird clanking, like a ghost, in the smoke somewhere behind her.

April threw open the door and reached fresh cold air at last. She took a couple of deep, life-giving breaths, and then dove back into the smoke to help Danny, who was half dragging, half carrying Karen through the front room.

They burst into the open air. April saw what had made the clanking and banging.

"No time . . ." Danny coughed. "Had to bring the whole traction gear with us." He carried chains, pulleys, metal bars and all. Now he bent

150

over Karen. "Unconscious," he muttered. "Don't know how long. She needs emergency treatment."

"What about the ski patrol stuff in the ski shack?" April cried. "At least there are blankets in there!"

Danny nodded, already taking deep breaths to restore oxygen to his lungs, and at the same time tilting Karen's head back and pinching her nose to begin mouth-to-mouth rescue breathing.

April raced for the ski shack. She dragged the ski patrol sled out of its closet and hurried back to them, pulling it behind her. While Danny breathed steadily into Karen's mouth, April tucked one of the warm brown blankets under and around her. She had managed to unhook the leg cast from the tangle of traction bars, and lower Karen's body to a normal position.

"Try for a pulse," Danny said quickly, between breaths.

April had been shown in the ski patrol first aid class how to lay her two fingers in the right spot on someone's inner wrist. Thump. . . thump. . . thump. . . She nodded a 'yes' to Danny. Karen's heart was beating. "Now please start breathing," April cried. "Oh Karen. . . please start breathing!"

It seemed they were there for a hundred years, in the quiet snow with Karen's still, white body and Danny rhythmically bending to blow air into her lungs and straightening to take another breath.

Suddenly, Karen's chest gave a great heave. She twisted away from Danny's grip on her nose and began to cough. Danny, still kneeling beside her, helped her to sit up with an arm around her shoulder until the coughing fit was better, and held her hand.

April sat back on her heels and watched the look of joy and relief spread over Danny's face like a sunrise. She felt it herself. They'd won!

"Let's get her on the sled and over to the ski shack," Danny said at last. "We can light the oil stove and keep her warm in there."

Karen moaned and held tight to Danny, her face buried in his down ski jacket, still coughing

"Come on," he said gently, "Think I'm going to *carry* you with that cast on your leg? You must weigh a hundred kilos!" Karen made a sound that was half a sob and half a laugh. Danny grinned at April over Karen's head. April was thinking of the awful trip down the stairs when Danny had carried not only Karen and the cast, but half a tonne of traction equipment! At last Karen let go of his coat and they wrapped her body snugly on the ski patrollers' sled and towed her up to the ski shack.

It was only when they had her safely inside and lit the oil stove that they thought of the lodge. "There's nothing we can do," muttered Danny when April tugged at his sleeve and pointed out the window at the lodge roof, where smoke was still pouring into the air. "There's no fire department close enough to come, even if we *could* get inside to phone, which we can't."

April had never heard of such a thing. No fire department! But she realized it was true. Even if the trucks came from the nearest town, they wouldn't get there in time to do any good.

Anyway, their first concern was for Karen. The ski patrol equipment included a fast sterno stove for making hot tea, and they knew this was what was needed. The danger now was that Karen's body would go into shock — they must get her warm. They pulled the fibreglass sled up as close to the stove as they could, and Danny took off his jacket to wrap around her shivering body.

"You'll be all right, you'll be all right," he murmured, as she started to cry.

"I'm okay," she nodded, sobbing. "But, oh, Danny! The smoke woke me up, and the chimney was roaring, and I couldn't get free, and I thought no one would come."

April could picture the terrifying scene too clearly. She shuddered and moved closer to the stove. Danny had pushed Karen's arms into the sleeves of his jacket and zipped it up, and now they wrapped another brown wool blanket loosely around her.

"And I started choking... and everything got black." Karen looked up at them. "I thought I would never wake up, never see Dad or Mom or you... or anything again!" April tucked the blanket closely around Karen's bare feet, giving it a hug as she did so.

"And here's my ugly face, same as ever, eh?" Danny said, smiling. "You're going to be fine now, soon as we can get something hot into you! Where are your mom and dad?" He looked at April. The same thought had occurred to both of them. How had Uncle Neil and Aunt Nora come to leave Karen alone like that?

"They got a phone call. From the bank, I

think, or maybe the lawyer. Both of them had to be there by three o'clock. I said I'd be okay. I was sleepy. . . I didn't know there'd be a fire."

Danny nodded. "That's the trouble with those darn airtight fireplaces. The creosote builds up inside the chimney. You can get a chimney fire any time. Sometimes they don't do much damage, but if the wood near the chimney catches on fire. . ."

"Will the lodge burn down?" whispered Karen.

Danny shook his head anxiously, "Don't know," he answered. "I don't think the roof will catch, too much snow. But inside, there's a lot of dry old wood in the place."

April stood up quickly. Something had been worrying away in the back of her mind through all this emergency, and Danny's last words brought it sharply into focus. Blue Suit and his greasy friend Bill. . . talking when they thought no one could hear them! Something about the wood being dry. . . and the place being a *firetrap*! She tugged on Danny's shoulder. "I think I know how the fire started."

He looked up, puzzled. "Sure, I just told you. . . creosote in the chimney. Hey, you're shivering too. Let's get this tea thing going."

"No. . . I. . . " April started to say, and then decided that this wasn't a good time to tell Danny or Karen what she knew. But oh, Uncle Neil, she thought, hurry back! Don't let those rats burn down Snowbird. I know! I know what happened!

"I'm going to run out to the highway and flag down a car," Danny said, after the hot tea was poured, steaming, into blue enamel mugs. He took a couple of quick gulps and headed for the shack door.

"You haven't got your jacket," April protested.

"That's why I'm going to run!" Danny grinned.

"I'll go!" April said.

"We've already proved I'm faster," Danny said. He turned to look at Karen, his face suddenly serious. "Listen, Karen, we were racing from the road, April and I—she saw the fire, and the first thing she thought of was you, alone in the loft. What more can I say?" He shrugged his eloquent Danny shrug, and dashed out.

April shut the door tight behind him and came to sit back down by the stove. Karen was crying again, big tears running down her cheeks and splashing into her mug of tea. It must be the shock, April thought, wondering what to do. "Does it hurt?" she asked. She gently pulled the hot mug of tea out of Karen's hands and set it on the floor so it wouldn't spill.

"I'm okay," Karen sobbed, suddenly gripping April's hand in her two cold ones. "I'm just so glad you came. And so sorry . . ."

April threw both arms around the big bundle of blankets and coat and hugged hard. "I'm sorry, too," she said into the bundle. "About your leg, and coming here and spoiling things for you, and . . ."

"No!" Karen cried. "You don't understand. It's not your fault. I . . . I don't know what was wrong with me! I was all mixed up in my head.

I've always had my parents and Snowbird all to myself. I was afraid. I didn't know how to share them. And Danny! You know how it is at the races, with all those rich kids in a gang? But I never cared if we were from a club that no one ever heard of. . . because there were always the two of us . . . and we were together!"

"It's all right," April said. "You don't have to explain." She felt as though the big weight she'd been carrying had suddenly been jerked off her shoulders.

"No!" Karen went on, looking into April's eyes with her large blue ones. "I have to tell you! I was jealous—I was afraid Danny liked you better."

April stared back. It was hard to believe. Karen . . . the blond goddess, the champion . . . jealous! Of her! But it was true, Danny had sometimes made a fuss over her. Like the time she'd hurt her shoulder, and when she'd been fighting with Karen. She saw clearly all of a sudden how that must have looked to Karen.

"I think," April said slowly, "I think he just feels sorry for me." Danny was naturally kind and sympathetic, and knew how it felt to be an outsider. But April found herself wishing that Danny didn't pity her. "I've played up to him sometimes," she admitted, "to make him feel sorrier. He really admires you, Karen!" she went on. "He thinks you're wonderful. He . . . he was coming today to see you!"

"I know!" A great big happy smile lit up Karen's exhausted face. "They say a true friend is always there when you need him most. I guess I don't need any more proof than that!"

157

===========
CHAPTER EIGHTEEN
===========

Almost Murder

========================

While they huddled by the stove, waiting for help to arrive, April and Karen talked. They sorted out the last four months as if it were a messy cupboard they both shared; they threw out the garbage, the bitterness and envy, and put the good stuff where they could reach it easily. They both loved Aunt Nora and Uncle Neil and Snowbird, and now they shared a passion for skiing.

"You feel like you're a bird soaring on the wind down the hill," April said trying to describe how she felt.

Karen nodded. "I thought I didn't want to live if I couldn't ski," she said.

"You'll ski again!" April cried, hugging her cousin.

"I know. But it's as though I woke up from a big nightmare and could see how lucky I am just to be here," Karen said, looking around the shadowy old ski shack.

April glanced up at the darkening window, hoping it wouldn't be suddenly lit by a sheet of flame from the burning lodge; hoping somebody had picked Danny up on the highway and that help would come soon. Ten minutes ticked by, then fifteen, then twenty. . . Karen's weary head drooped on her shoulder.

At last the door burst open. There were Uncle Neil, Aunt Nora, and Danny—wearing Uncle Neil's old truck parka. Then there were hugs of joy and relief.

"Someone drove me to the gas station," Danny explained, "and we picked up Mr. Hearst on the CB radio."

"Can't tell if the fire's out," Uncle Neil said "there's still an awful lot of smoke. If you're okay, Danny, let's try and get inside."

"I'm with you, Mr. Hearst," Danny said. "But I really thought those two girls would have everything under control by now." He grinned wickedly at the two figures huddled close and dashed after Uncle Neil.

An hour later the last smouldering ceiling beam had been smothered in foam from the big fire extinguisher Uncle Neil had borrowed from the gas station. Snowbird Mountain Lodge had been saved.

Uncle Neil, April and Danny stood in the bright moonlight, gazing in weary relief at the old log building. Suddenly, April remembered what had been bothering her. "Uncle Neil," she said, tugging at his parka, "remember when Mr. Delorac and that other man were in the lodge? They were talking about it being just a big old firetrap—how easily it would burn! Maybe..."

Uncle Neil turned and stared at her. "Are you sure?"

"I'm *sure*!" April nodded. "I heard them through the wall."

Uncle Neil looked very angry. "All right," he said, "we won't touch anything until the police have had a good look tomorrow morning. Now let's get some sleep in the ski shack. It'll be crowded but cozy."

"I always heard that things looked better in the morning," April groaned, looking at the ruined living room. "Well, it's not true. They look worse!"

It was a fact. In the clear light of day, Snowbird Mountain Lodge was a wreck. Every wall and windowpane was blackened and streaked with smoke and soot. The whole place smelled terrible; the stale smoke smell was deep into carpets and curtains and furniture. Even the cold cereal they tried to eat for breakfast tasted smoky!

"What's the use of cleaning all this up," Aunt Nora said hopelessly, "if we're just going to be evicted by the bank next Wednesday?"

"Did the police find anything, Uncle Neil?" April asked.

"The sheet metal that protected the upstairs floor beams was twisted and pulled away from around the chimney, where it goes through the floor." Uncle Neil nodded. "The police aren't sure if it was the heat from the fire that did it," he went on grimly, "but I'm sure it wasn't. Someone pulled that metal protector away so that if we did have a chimney fire, the whole lodge would go up. It's a good thing April hit the log beams with some of the foam from our little fire extinguisher. That slowed the fire down. Even so, I figure ten minutes more and this whole place might have been in flames."

"But how could they be sure you'd have a

160

chimney fire?" asked Danny. "They don't happen that often."

"That's what I've been wondering," Uncle Neil said, looking up at the chimney. "It's very easy to start one, you know. Just take out the plug from the bottom of the stovepipe, put in a piece of lighted paper, and bingo! There's your fire!"

"But who . . . ?"

"Mr. Smoothie Blue Suit, that's who!" April cried. "Oh, Uncle Neil, I know that's what he and that guy Bill were planning, the day I saw them." April had given her story and a description of 'Bill' to the police officers.

"Neil!" said Aunt Nora suddenly. "Could they have known we both had to go to the lawyer's office yesterday afternoon?"

"It's possible, I guess," Uncle Neil said. "But what about Karen? They wouldn't set a fire with Karen here!"

"They wouldn't know she *was* here, unless they went upstairs. They'd think . . . oh, Neil! They'd think she was at school."

"But she'd hear them, surely . . ." Uncle Neil said slowly.

"She was asleep," April remembered. "She said she took a pain pill because her leg hurt; and she didn't wake up until the smoke was really thick."

"But why would they want to burn the lodge?" Danny asked. A feeling of horror was dawning on all four of them.

Uncle Neil took a deep breath. "I suppose," he said, "our developer friend could have set this fire to reduce Snowbird Mountain's value when the bank puts it up for sale in a few days. The bank gets my fire insurance money, so they're happy. Then the bank sells the land to Delorac and his company for a song. The land's all they want; they don't care about this old place," he gestured around the bleak looking lodge.

"Oh Neil!" murmured Aunt Nora, shivering.

"That's arson—setting fires deliberately," Uncle Neil went on. "But this, if we're right—this was almost murder!" He put his arm around his wife's shaking shoulders. "It's all right now, Nora, but I don't think we'd better mention any of this to Karen. She's had enough shocks for a while."

April and Danny nodded in agreement.

"Maybe we should think of moving into a motel, Neil," Aunt Nora said. "It's so uncomfortable for Karen in the ski shack, and she has to keep her leg in traction and... I want her safe." April could see Aunt Nora had been badly frightened. Her face looked small and grey. "I mean, we'll have to anyway in a few days..."

"Listen Nora," Uncle Neil said, turning her face towards him. "I'm going to have that loft floor fixed by tonight, and Karen can move back into her own room. Those thugs have tried to bully us out and bribe us out, and I'll be darned if I'm going to let them *burn* us out of Snowbird Mountain. It's our home, and we're going to stay right here!"

Hurrah, Uncle Neil! April wanted to shout.

"April," Uncle Neil turned to her, "I have a big job for you. Can you clear all your stuff—yours and Karen's—out of the loft this morning? I need space to work."

"Sure," April said. "What'll I do with it?"

Aunt Nora shook her shoulders and seemed to gather herself together. "Put everything that needs to be washed into green plastic bags," she said, handing April half a dozen. "Throw out whatever you can. The rest . . . we'll just put . . . somewhere!" She waved her hands helplessly at the mess.

"While April's cleaning the loft, Danny," Uncle Neil said, "would you give me a hand digging some new boards out of the drift by the woodshed?"

"*Oui!*" Danny said. "Don't fall through that hole in the floor, Ape!" he teased, pointing up at the circular hole where Uncle Neil had already cut away the charred loft floor.

April went slowly up the curving log staircase. The smell of smoke was stronger here, and it was cold. It doesn't seem like our room anymore, April thought, as she started to work. She sniffed Karen's quilt and coughed. The smoke smell was awful!

She stripped the beds, stuffing blankets, sheets and quilts into bags. Then she emptied the dresser drawers and took all the stuff off the tops. She did Karen's first because it was so much neater. Karen's sweetgrass box full of barrettes; her eye shadow collection and special ski moisturizer for skiing; her Mexican wallet; the blue pottery bowls that she'd made at school — it all went carefully into a separate bag.

All of Karen's things have that specialness, April thought. Like her. She felt warm suddenly with the thought that now she would be able to

163

share that specialness; she'd help Karen set all this up again when the loft got fixed. There'd be a lot of things she could do to help until Karen's leg was better.

Then she turned to her own dresser. What a contrast! she thought with a grimace. Mess city! I guess I learned it from Dad all right—just put everything in a big pile and sooner or later the thing you need will percolate to the surface.

She paused over a box of junk in the top drawer. That was the one box she'd managed to save from Aunt Nora's cleaning spree when her aunt had moved her out of Vancouver.

Suddenly that old life came flooding back to her as she sat cross-legged on the floor with the box on her lap. Old letters, overdue bills with big red stamps, report cards from her old school, recipes from magazines and photograph negatives—the important and the unimportant, all cheerfully jumbled together. 'The Swamp Box', Dad had called it, she remembered; it had always gone with them from apartment to apartment.

I guess I'll just throw it all out, April thought, scrabbling through the box. It would take all day to sort it.

But she hated to dump 'The Swamp Box' into a garbage bag. It didn't seem right somehow. Her dad, that hopeless collector, would have saved it. Never sorted it, April thought with a grin. Just saved it. She picked up a long, unopened envelope with a window in the front. 'Premium notice', she read. Probably another old bill he never opened. The word 'Insurance' caught her eye; they'd all been talking about how the fire insurance on Snowbird Lodge would all go to the bank now.

She turned the envelope over and tore it open. It was a bill all right, for $182.50. That was a lot of money — no wonder this one ended up in the swamp! April read the official sounding words, 'Whole Life Policy of twenty-five thousand dollars'.

April stared at the bill. She leaped to her feet.

"Uncle Neil!" she shouted.

Luckily, he was coming in the back door with a load of wood, because April tripped on the Swamp Box and went sailing through the open space in the floor. He dropped the wood with a clatter as she landed in his arms, clutching a long piece of paper.

"Hey Ape! I told you to watch for that hole in the floor," Danny said, coming in after Uncle Neil.

"Uncle Neil! What does this mean?" She tried to straighten the crumpled paper and hold it so he could see. "Twenty-five . . . thousand . . . "

Uncle Neil set April down. He reached for the paper and read it. Then he looked at April, his face turning red and white at the same time.

"Where did you find this?" he said.

"In the Swamp . . . I mean in a box of junk from Vancouver," April said eagerly, scanning her uncle's face. She wished he'd talk, instead of just staring at the paper.

"What is it?" Danny asked.

"A premium notice. For a life insurance policy that your dad had, April. But look at the date! This bill is two and a half years overdue!" He shook his head. "Life insurance is not much good if you don't pay the premiums." He scrumpled the thin paper into a ball.

"Let me see that." Aunt Nora caught it as he tossed it away. "Do you have the envelope, April, with an address or telephone number?"

"What are you going to do?" Uncle Neil said, as April tore off upstairs. "It's just an old, out-of-date policy, Nora."

"Make a phone call," Aunt Nora said.

When Aunt Nora came back from making the phone call in the kitchen, there was a strange look on her face. She sat down on the bottom step of the loft stairs and looked up at the three waiting faces. "It was an old policy all right," she said. "Thirteen years old. And made out to me! You weren't even born, April, when your dad took out this insurance. But the man said . . . " She looked up at Uncle Neil and the strange look suddenly became a wide smile. "He said Michael probably intended to change the beneficiary to April but never got around to it. That would be like my brother," she chuckled.

"Beneficiary?" April asked. "What's that?"

"The person who gets the money," Aunt Nora said. "The agent I talked to said — I don't understand — but I think he said it doesn't matter that Michael didn't pay the premiums for the last two years. They'll just subtract those premium payments from the total amount. Neil! This twenty-five thousand dollars is ours. It's Snowbird's. Oh thank you, Michael! And thank you, April!" She looked at April and her face was like a rainbow!

CHAPTER NINETEEN

The Final Challenge

Afterwards, everyone kept saying how surprised they were that the twenty-five thousand dollar life insurance policy should have turned up just then . . . when money was the most important thing.

April didn't say anything, but somehow she wasn't surprised. It was how she and her father had always lived. Money wasn't important, except when you had to have it, and then it usually turned up.

And they all kept saying what a miracle it was that the premium notice hadn't gotten thrown out, when April was cleaning. April knew that you could be too eager a thrower-outer. The important thing was that she'd been upstairs by herself with 'The Swamp Box'; with a chance to remember and think about Vancouver and her dad. She didn't believe that she would ever have thrown the insurance bill away.

"It was just waiting for the right time to come to the top of the pile," she explained to Danny.

"Uh...what do you mean?" He looked confused.

"You know, like the way your baseball mitt just hangs in the back of the coat closet all winter, but suddenly when spring comes, it falls off the shelf one day and hits you on the head!"

"I never noticed," said Danny, rubbing his head.

"That's because you don't live in a properly organized household," laughed April. She felt very happy. It was as if Dad had somehow managed to reach out and help them save the place he had helped to build so long ago. And now people would stop saying what a crazy mixed-up life he had led, as if he'd never done anything right. The mortgage on Snowbird was paid off, and there would be enough money left for lots of extras, like new skis for Danny for the finals of the Challenge Cup in North Bay.

By Friday morning, when Danny and Uncle Neil left for the race, Snowbird Mountain Lodge was empty and echoing. All the furniture, rugs and drapes had been sent away to be cleaned, and the wall logs and floors scrubbed clean and shiny. Karen's bed was back upstairs in the bare loft with its new floor; but now sunshine seemed to fill the room, and there was lots of traffic up and down the curving stairway.

"Tell Mom not to put that dumb blanket back up," Karen said, as April came up with a cup of 'red zinger' cinnamon tea for her. "It looks so much better without it, don't you think?"

"If you can stand my mess!" April grinned as she handed Karen the hot spicy tea.

"It's not so bad," Karen looked down the loft at April's lumpy bunk, and the patch of sunny blue sky in the gable window. "Oh look at that day! I hope it's like this in North Bay!" She cradled her mug of tea between her palms and lay with her head thrown back on her pillow looking at the one piece of the outdoors she could see, her eyes far away.

"Aunt Nora said they'd phone tomorrow night and tell us how Danny was doing," April said, knowing how much Karen must be longing to be there, racing down the hill to the cheers of the crowd.

When Uncle Neil did phone the next night, Aunt Nora came tearing up the stairs, breathless, with the news. "Two golds!" she cried. "He won the slalom in the morning and the giant slalom in the afternoon. Neil says Danny's really nervous about the downhill race tomorrow, but Neil thinks he has a chance!"

"More than a chance!" Karen cried, her eyes shining. "He can do it if he just doesn't lose his nerve. In downhill racing, you've just got to point your skis and fly — and not worry about falling."

She stopped suddenly. "Look who's giving advice," she sighed, looking ruefully up at her cast, hanging from the 'traction contraption' as Danny called it. She looked from April to Aunt Nora and back to April again. "I did lose my nerve when I fell, you know. I suddenly thought, *I'm not going to make it* . . . and WIPE OUT!"

April looked at her cousin with admiration.

This was a new Karen, fearless and determined like before, but with a splinter of ice gone from her heart.

Sunday brought more good news and a surprise, for behind Uncle Neil's gold pick-up, the blue van of the Northern Divisional ski team came rolling into the Snowbird parking lot, with John Bukowski's smiling face at the wheel.

"I came to see Karen," he said as he hopped out of the van, "and this famous hill that produces so many champions. Three gold medals," he said, raising Danny's arm aloft, "*and* the boy's Juvenile championship. How's that for one weekend?"

They all trooped up to the loft and perched around Karen's bed. "I saved a spot on my cast for the champ's autograph," Karen said, handing Danny a pen. "Just sign right here on my knee."

While Danny signed, John Bukowski came around the bed to take Karen's hand. "We missed you today," he said, smiling down at her. "The girls were all asking how you were."

"I'll bet they didn't miss my competition in the races," Karen said bravely, trying to smile back. "Uh . . . who won, the girl's Juvenile championship? Who's going on to Fortress Mountain?"

April caught Uncle Neil and Aunt Nora's quick exchange of glances. They all knew what a tough moment this was for Karen.

"Well, Tina came out on top this year," John said, "but that's not what I came to talk to you about." He patted her hand. "I thought I'd like to tell you in person whom I've chosen for the Divisional Team next year." He turned to Danny.

"Danny, I'd like to put you on the 'C' team. I could put you higher after this weekend's performance, but I'd like to give you a little while to work up. If I put you on the 'A' team you'll be expected to do *very* well next year in the Provincial and even Canadian races, and you'll find it a big jump to that kind of competition. Bigger hills, artificial snow — it's a different world."

Danny was looking so thrilled April was sure he wasn't even hearing all this. He'd made the team. *That* was enough!

"And Karen," She looked up at the coach, bracing herself for disappointment. "You've had a tough break — if you'll pardon the awful pun." He smiled at her. "But I've talked to your doctor, and he says you'll be skiing next year as well as ever... maybe better. That's great news. Some injuries are worse," he pounded his own thigh, "and we never get back to racing." Aunt Nora nodded sympathetically and April, Danny and Karen stared at him. So that's why John was a coach, and not on the Olympic team.

"Mom never told me you'd broken your leg," Karen blurted, raising herself on one elbow.

"It's not something I generally like my skiers to know," John smiled. "It gets them thinking about injury, and there's no use in that."

"So," he went on, "I'd like to put you on the training squad, Karen. That means you'll come with us to the dryland and on-snow training camp out West next fall. If you look good I'll be able to move you up to the 'D' team, and we can go from there."

Karen looked as though she were about to

171

burst. She threw herself around John Bukowski's neck and rattled her traction contraption dangerously. "Watch it!" Danny cried. "That cast is a lethal weapon!"

"And now," said Aunt Nora, beaming, "that you've made us all so happy, John, it's time for my patient to get some rest. It's past ten." She tucked the quilts up around Karen as they all said good night and disappeared down the log staircase. April was the last to go.

"I can't believe it," Karen sighed happily, snuggling down in bed. "I've got to get better fast."

"I bet I know what you're going to dream about tonight," April grinned as she switched off the light and followed the others downstairs.

They all gathered in front of the living room fire. The furniture was back from the cleaners and grouped in its old familiar way. John and Uncle Neil sat in the easy chairs, April stretched out on the couch, Danny was cross-legged on the rug, and Aunt Nora leaned against the warm bricks, with the firelight on her face.

"I hear there's another Hearst champion coming up," John said, crinkling up his eyes at April. "Sorry, I guess you're not actually a Hearst . . ."

"She's a Martineau!" Aunt Nora said proudly.

"The kids have a day off school tomorrow," Uncle Neil said. "Why don't I start the tow in the morning, and April can show you the hill?"

"What a life!" John said. "Wake up in the morning and the hill's right outside your front door. Ski all day, and then come in to this." He gestured around the warm cozy room. "Far away from the city, in your own wilderness of snow!"

The others around the fire exchanged amused looks. They wouldn't tell John what it had *really* been like sometimes that winter. Or other winters — when there *was* no snow.

April was so excited about taking John Bukowski up Snowbird Mountain the next morning, that she was almost disappointed when a police officer showed up with the news about Blue Suit at last. All the excitement of the past few days had shoved thoughts of the ski developers far to the back of her mind.

"We're bringing in a certain young man for questioning," the officer said. "He's wanted for arson already in Quebec. Do you think you could spot your 'Bill' in a group of other men?"

"Of course I could!" said April. And then, seeing the amusement on the officer's face, ". . . at least I'm pretty sure I could."

"What about Mr. Delorac, April's Mr. Blue Suit?" Uncle Neil asked. "He's the one I'd like to see behind bars!"

"A much bigger fish." The officer shook his head. "And much more slippery, I'm afraid."

"Slimy," said April.

The officer grinned. "You're a young lady with definite opinions, aren't you?" he said. "Our friend Mr. Delorac seems to have charmed everyone else around this area."

"Do you mean," said Aunt Nora, joining the conversation, "that Mr. Delorac wasn't the real thing?"

"We don't know that." The officer shook his head. "He may have been representing big European business interests, the way he said." He looked at them. "All we know is that we can't find hide nor hair of Mr. Delorac *or* his friend..."

"Beige Suit," said April quickly.

"And this scheme for a ski resort seems to have vanished into thin air," the police officer went on. "Nobody really knows anything about it."

They all stared at each other.

"I don't care," cried Aunt Nora. "He's gone, that's the main thing! They're not going to put us out of business. There's not going to be any guest chalets, and million-dollar lodge, and planeloads of tourists..."

"I don't know about that," Uncle Neil chuckled. "I might just do it myself... put in a revolving restaurant on the top of Snowbird... and a swimming pool... and..."

The police officer must have wondered, April thought afterward, why they all collapsed, laughing, on the lunch counter.

Other Books in the *JEANPAC* Series:

THE GHOST OF PIRATE WALK

Jerry Williams

THE MYSTERY OF THE GHOSTLY RIDERS

Lynn Manuel

THE DNA DIMENSION   Carol Matas

THE OTHER ELIZABETH   Karleen Bradford

I WISH THERE WERE UNICORNS

Karleen Bradford

KIRSTINE AND THE VILLAINS   Elfreida Read

RACE AGAINST THE DARK   Elfreida Read

CHAMPIONS   Marjorie Holland

SKATE LIKE THE WIND   Joan Ford